OUTSIDER

OUTSIDER

A Sean Colbeth Mystery

CHRISTOPHER JANSMANN

Christopher H. Jansmann

ISBN-13: 9780578829135 (Kindle)
ISBN-13: 9798585271588 (Paperback)
ISBN-13: 9781087939988 (Hardcover)

Cover design by Christopher Jansmann

Library of Congress Control Number: 2021926084

Printed in the United States of America

First Printing, 2021

For Paula

My muse, my world, my everything

Contents

One

The bullet shattered the window of the driver's side door.

I threw my hands protectively above my head and tried to wedge myself into the front of the departmental SUV, thankful the auto safety glass simply created rounded shards that rolled off the back of my winter jacket. A second bullet whistled over my head as what was left of the windshield cascaded over me, followed closely by a third bullet that implanted itself with a definitive *thunk* in the rear seatback.

Scrambling as best as I could through the slick glass shards, I pressed myself down into the wheel well behind the engine compartment, playing the odds that the metallic mass would offer some semblance of safety from the crazed fury I'd apparently unleashed with my attempt to serve an Eminent Domain eviction to Bethesda Thompkins. There were all sorts of parts to my position as Chief of Police in Windeport that I tended to dislike, none more than the incredibly emotional separation of people and what *had* been their property; it didn't help that this particular situation was one I'd disagreed with on a personal level from the start. For Bethesda and her unbroken five generations of dairy farming were being shoved aside in favor of a timeshare development associated with what passed for a ski resort in the county.

Far more than the recent murder I had worked, the town had cleanly divided itself between those who wanted the economic shot–in–the–arm the project would bring to our fading village and the rest that were aghast at the casting aside of nearly a century old family business that was still successful. As I carefully poked my head around the edge of the door, I was having a hard time reminding myself of which side I was on, for despite my personal feelings in the matter, the Village Council had embraced the dream of a financial windfall the developer was promising and had made my department the efficient agent in expediting matters.

In short, I had unwillingly become the very public face of the situation.

Peering into the early gloom of the winter evening, I caught the shadow of someone behind the smashed window the shots had come from, and ducked a fraction of a second before something sailed through the space I'd just been in. Crouching again, I looked toward the slightly darker smudge in the snowbank five or so feet away from me. It had been my Glock or my iPhone when Bethesda had taken her first shot at me; sadly, the iPhone had lost the battle. Without it, though, my options were somewhat limited. Not that it mattered: given how good a shot the farmer was, it might as well have been ten miles away.

Shit, I thought. *Of all the times not to have a partner.*

The metal of the Glock was icy cold against the bare skin of my hand; peeking above the door slightly, I tried to gauge if my antagonist had paused to wait me out or had simply given up and gone back to watching *Jeopardy!* I let a minute go to three, and grimly smiled at the thought that even if she *had* somehow killed me, Bethesda was in no hurry to look at my corpse. At five minutes, the squishy coldness of my dress slacks from having to kneel in the slush of the driveway became irritating enough to prod me into action.

That, and I was missing dinner with my girlfriend.

Taking a deep breath, I threw myself toward the snowbank and with my free hand started to search in the darkness for my phone while I kept my eyes and the Glock trained on the wraparound front porch. As my fingers grew numb, they hit the hard case of the phone and yanked it out of the mushy snow; staying crouched, I edged toward the back of the SUV and then kept behind it. Wiping as much of the slush off the case I as could against my slacks, I quickly dialed 9–1–1.

"9–1–1, please state—"

"Emily, it's Sean. I need backup at the Thompkins place *now*."

Without missing a beat, I heard my night operator urgently call into the multi-band radio; in mere moments, she'd put my S.O.S. out across both our own patrol officers and any State or Sherriff units that might happen to be close at hand. Sliding around the edge of the SUV's bumper, I scanned the lighted windows of the front when Emily came back on. "Lydia is four minutes out; might have a State Trooper there in fifteen."

"I'll take what I can get," I said as I pulled back. "Get ahold of Gertrude and roll an ambulance, too."

"Are you hurt?"

"No," I said, "but I don't have a great feeling about how this is going to end."

"Got it. Stay safe, Chief."

"Oh, you're not getting rid of me that easy," I replied as I ended the call.

Staying in a crouch that my Academy instructor would have been proud of, I slunk along the edge of the SUV and tried to ignore how much damage her barrage was going to cost the department. My budget hadn't included so much as new light bulbs that year, so it would take some sweet talking to get the funds to offset what insurance didn't cover. A quick sprint put me behind a small stone wall that ran along the shoveled path to the porch; creeping along it, I could hear the dulcet tones of Alex Trebek as he guided the contestants through the final stages of whatever round they were in. I wasn't a fan of game shows per se, or television for that matter; prepping for the Olympics as a teen had left a massive hole in my understanding of pop culture of any kind. All I knew was that something had enthralled the septuagenarian enough to momentarily forget about me out there in her foreyard. It also didn't hurt that she had a touch of dementia, though that didn't appear to affect her gunslinging skills.

What a cruel, cruel disease, I thought as I crept up the short steps to the porch. The drapes were flapping out of what was left of one of the tall farmhouse windows along with smells of boiled okra and some sort of fish. *How it randomly robs these people of everything but leaves some things untouched is the worst cut of all.*

Keeping my Glock up, I put a hand to the screen door and carefully pulled it open; the massive wooden front door was cracked open slightly, and I edged a foot through it. Slowly, very slowly, I pushed through, opening it wide enough to get a good line of sight on the long sitting room beyond. A classic tube–based television with rabbit ears to match sat on a low table by the stone fireplace; an easy chair had it's back to me and was next to an L–shaped couch topped with white doily–like things. The okra smell was nearly intolerable.

I could just see the very top of Bethesda's gray bun over the edge of the easy chair; my unease went up a notch when it became apparent her gun wasn't visible. Swallowing, and wishing I'd not left my bulletproof vest back at the station, I slowly stood.

"Bethesda?"

"I can't do this anymore," came the muted reply.

I moved toward her. "Bethesda, let's talk about this," I said softly and with what I hoped was an encouraging voice. "I can overlook the fact you put a few holes in my truck—"

The movement was so swift, and so unexpected from someone I'd assumed would be less decisive, I had no chance to grab her arm before she pressed her gun to her temple; the sound of the shot reverberated through the cloistered space almost as fast as the splatter of crimson and white ghosted out over the hardwood floor. In the fraction of a second it took me to reach her – or what was left of her – Bethesda's arm had dropped as her body slumped sideways over the arm of the chair, the gun clattering to the floor a few feet from the stack of *TV Guides* dating back several months.

Kneeling next to her, I shook my head at the scene as the sound of approaching sirens came through the shattered window. Rates of suicide had been on the increase in the state, especially among the older population, but Windeport had been thankfully bucking the trend until very recently; still, two deaths in a village of our size in less than a year was not going to go over well at the next Village Meeting.

Shit.

Two

It was never good when the current chair of the Village Council paid a personal visit. Though I had quite a bit of respect for the retired dentist, Doug Hansen was as political a creature as they came; meeting with me privately would keep the session off the official record and out of what passed for our local paper. Coming to the office, though, would create its own waves and send a significant message to my staff – and to me, which at the end of the day, was truly the motivation.

"So, now we have three problems."

I sipped at my coffee. "How do you figure?"

Doug sighed and twisted the coffee I'd given him in his hands. Near as I could tell, about the only thing he'd taken from the mug was its heat. "We're still dealing with the aftermath of your investigation last fall," he said, obliquely referring to the Pelletier case and the civil defamation suit that the prime suspect had brought against Windeport, despite Dr. Yvette Bedard being quite properly incarcerated as a result of her actions. "The legal fees alone have depleted what reserves the Village had, and with our insurance carrier pushing for a settlement, we could still be on the hook for a substantial amount of cash."

"Settle?" I frowned. "What is there to settle *over*? She was convicted."

"Who knows," Doug replied. "But our lawyers – and those from the insurance company – think it best to make it all go away." He paused again. "There are a number of points being negotiated still, and one of them is your status with the department."

I stared at him for a moment, digesting his words. "That vindictive—"

"Exactly," Doug smiled tiredly as he cut me off with a wave of his hand. "Up to this point, it had been off the table, but once news hit about what went down over to the Thompkins place, our lawyers – and the insurance company – think the other side can make a better case that you're a loose cannon."

"Me?" I nearly choked on my coffee. "A loose cannon? Have they even *looked* at my record?"

"It doesn't matter," Doug sighed again. "You've been in this business long enough to know what a solid lawyer can do in front of a persuadable jury. Besides, they're more worried about what this will cost their shareholders than what happens here in the Village."

"I can't believe I'm hearing this," I said tightly, feeling a slight bubble of anger. "The Council has never given me *any* impression that I've not been fulfilling my duties properly."

"That was before we had two deaths in less than six months," Doug pointed out.

"Are you *serious*?" I replied. "Is that the official position of the Village Council? That major crime has increased under my watch and I therefore have to go?"

"No," Doug said uneasily. "Not exactly."

"Then what? *Exactly.*"

The Chair hedged. "We're not used to such high profile... situations," he started. "While you handled the case this fall extremely well, the subsequent lawsuit has exposed some... flaws... in your methods. And now, with this incident with Bethesda, running up there like it was the Old West without backup———"

"I'm shorthanded at the moment," I reminded him through clenched teeth.

"Why is that, exactly?" Doug asked pointedly. "Why have you not filled the position left vacant by Detective Korsokovach?"

I shifted slightly. "That's the third then, isn't it?"

"Yes," Doug said. "The case can be made that through your own actions, or inactions more properly, the staffing situation here in the department led to Bethesda's death."

"That's simply not true!"

"Can you honestly tell me," Doug said softly, "it wouldn't have gone differently if you'd had someone with you? That Bethesda would now, today, be getting the assistance she needs in some memory care ward in Bangor instead of lying in the morgue in Augusta?"

At that odd moment, I was startled to realize I'd drained my coffee in the short time we'd been talking. Standing, I came around my battleship of a desk to the Keurig on the sideboard, selected a K–cup, slid the mug beneath the spigot and then watched as the dark liquid begin to fill the void. Doug wasn't wrong, for I knew exactly what I'd been thinking while being pinned down at the farm; it was no less excusable knowing Bethesda had been diminished by her dementia. Why *had* I assumed she would have been the meek grandmotherly persona of a prior decade, despite being well aware that even on a good day, her medications could barely allow her to remember how a light switch worked?

As the steam wafted away from the rising surface of what had to have been my tenth or eleventh cup of the day, I knew I had been off my game for months. I wasn't a risk taker by nature, and though I wasn't opposed to slightly bending the rules, I'd never *ever* considered myself to be reckless. Tossing the used K–cup to the trash, though, it seemed recent evidence was to the contrary.

"No," I replied slowly as I turned and leaned against the counter. "I can't, especially because I was acutely aware of the absence of a partner that night."

Doug nodded, and smiled slightly. "I think all of us understand why you've had trouble filling the spot. But dragging your feet has just complicated matters for everyone."

Sipping the hot coffee, I moved back behind my massive desk and settled in again. The bulk of the relic from another era seemed to accentuate the distance between us. "Am I being fired, then? As part of the settlement?"

"You really get to the point," he frowned and then looked away for a moment before continuing. "That's why I'm here in person. There was a motion made in Executive Session to accept the recommendations of our lawyers." Doug turned back and considered me; there was a trace of pain in his eyes, betraying his next words.

"I will be frank, Sean. I've known you for years now – hell, I was on the committee that recommended you for this position."

"I remember."

"I think you are an incredible asset to Windeport, one that we have significantly undervalued for too long. I managed to dodge this effort when the civil suit first hit us, but after Bethesda... I just don't have the votes to prevent them from cancelling your contract, simple as that. The best I could do was table the motion until our next meeting in an attempt to give myself time to twist an arm, or two." He looked away again.

"You're not confident you can."

"No." Doug stood. "At the end of the day, you are likely to wind up paying the price for a few Council members' lack of courage. And for that, I am truly sorry."

I smiled wryly as I stood myself. "I imagine there's not much I could do to dissuade the other members from following through?"

"It might be best for you to lay low for a bit, actually," Doug replied as he shrugged on his overcoat.

"You're suspending me," I observed.

Pulling on his knit cap, Doug shook his head. "Not officially." He sighed. "This is a small town, Chief. Honestly? For me to work my magic, I need a few days with you out of sight. Go upstate and camp. Visit your father in Florida. Do *something*, just not here in Windeport."

It occurred to me that time–in–position might have made me a bit complacent with respect to my job security; more alarming perhaps was how quickly my years of reliably solid service to the Village had been tossed aside for the sake of financial expedience. I supposed it was the downside to working for a political entity, one often beset by the whims of the people it purported to serve, though as I stood there, I was unsure *who* those were exactly. Staring at my cooling coffee for a moment, it now seemed naïve to have presumed it to be the citizens of the Village.

"All right," I said, looking back to Doug. "I'll find some way to keep out from underfoot."

"Good." Stepping toward the door to my office, he paused. "You're not as political as the rest of us, something that I feel makes you pretty damn amazing at what you do. But if you would permit me to offer a little advice?"

I shrugged. "Sure. Why not?"

"Patch up whatever has gone wrong between you and your cousin," he said. "It's not gone unnoticed that she, too, seems to have lost faith in you."

Three

I spent the next few days tidying up several minor cases I'd been working on and attempting to keep a lower-than-normal profile, going so far as to drive all the way to Augusta to do my grocery shopping in order to avoid running into anyone from Windeport. The two–hour roundtrip gave me plenty of time to consider my situation; while I had no intention of willingly leaving my post as Chief, it did seem prudent to assume it might not be a choice within my purview, happening a bit sooner than my retirement plan had intended. So, I worked my network of friends and former colleagues, putting feelers out for possibilities that could soften my landing if the unthinkable happened. Despite what I knew to be a stellar reputation within the law enforcement community, it did worry me that a formal dismissal could hurt any immediate chance of employment.

Two of my contacts I *didn't* reach out to, though.

I was reasonably certain that James Roberts, Captain of the Eastern District for the State Police would take me on in a heartbeat regardless of what transpired in Windeport. He'd been after me for years to join him, so calling him before I knew the outcome of the upcoming vote at the next Village Council seemed premature and possibly unfair. I respected him too much to get him that excited, so left him in my back pocket as a fallback plan.

The other contact had been steadfastly ignoring my text messages and voicemails since his departure the prior Thanksgiving. Taking it as a sign of where we currently stood with each other, I decided to put Vasily into the "pure desperation Hail Mary" part of my plan: if it all went to Hell, maybe he'd at least let me crash with him in sunny California for a few weeks to get over the worst of my professional pain.

My officers and civilian staff knew *something* was going on, but in true Maine fashion, opted to soldier on. Still, in ways large and small, they had telegraphed their support for me. While I'd inherited a few lifers from the former Chief, the rest had been part of my own recruiting efforts – not that it had been easy finding dedicated professionals to join a small outpost in one of the poorest counties in the state. I felt quite justified in my pride with respect to the low turnover. The undercurrent of backing took a bit of an edge off the entire enterprise.

Not having a number two, though, did make it difficult to take any sort of time off. Technically, there wasn't an official Assistant Chief position in my department, but Vasily had essentially become my de facto second in the eyes of the staff and Windeport writ large. I was sure that was why it had become problematic replacing him, for the vacant position, while blessed with a solid salary for that part of the state, was nonetheless for a senior investigator; I wanted to replace my right hand, but had yet to see an applicant that fit the bill. Experienced investigators? Absolutely, I'd interviewed seven so far.

My backup? None had come close.

At length, I found myself with all of my outstanding tidbits completed and no desire to begin anything new. Closing down the last of the reports I'd just finished reading, I closed the lid to my MacBook and swiveled my chair around to look out the massive window of my office. It appeared to be snowing again; large flakes were lazily descending from the overcast sky, creating a gentle white layer just thick enough to obscure the nastiness that appeared between storms. There was a certain sense of peace you could get from falling snow, and only one way to enjoy it. I impulsively decided I needed to take a walk.

It took but a moment to lace up my Bean Boots and then don my heavy winter jacket; gloves followed, and I tugged on a thermal knit cap as I pushed out through the front door of the station. The icy cold air was bracing as I trudged across the small parking lot and made for where I thought the sidewalk ordinarily would reside. With everything coated in unrelieved white, the only indication of its location was the slightly lower level of snow as befitted a previously shoveled walkway. Traffic along Route One was nonexistent and totally typical for that part of the calendar; as I carefully made my way up the street, it occurred to me that The Colonial had not panned out as the exotic all–season getaway Marriott had been hoping for. Whispers of staff downsizing and a possible sale had been rampant for weeks, calling into question the viability of the timeshare project Bethesda had died over. For if a five–star resort barely ten miles from the ski resort in question wasn't packing them in at the height of the season, why would an unaffiliated vacation property on the far side of town be more successful? While Brad Donohue had multiple successes under his belt, I had my doubts about the feasibility of the local real estate mogul's project.

Without intending to do so, I wandered past the old pharmacy, crossed the street by Calista's Bakery, and made my way to the ornate doors of Saint Catherine's By–The–Sea. They were unlocked as always, in keeping with the parish's longstanding practice of allowing visitors to the sanctuary at nearly any hour of the day. Stomping the worst of the snow out of my boots on the rubber mats, I crossed the vestibule toward the frosted glass doors of the inner chamber, the scent of incense heavy in the air, mixed with candle wax and fresh flowers.

Reaching to pull open one side, though, I stepped back immediately when it swung wide of its own accord, revealing the tall form of my cousin, Charlie O'Conner. She came to a dead stop a few feet from me, the look of surprise on her face likely mirroring my own. In the months since I'd hauled her to the station as a murder suspect in the Pelletier case, we'd made a point of avoiding each other; I was well aware that I had hurt her, deeply, but from my perspective, I'd only been doing my job. While it had become clear fairly quickly she'd not taken the same view of my actions, I'd been at a loss as to how to repair the damage.

A near constant presence in my life since I was four, I missed talking to Charlie. I wasn't sure if she'd intended to return hurt with hurt, for not seeing my nieces had been devastating over the holidays. Yet reconciling in any way had become all the harder the longer we went without talking.

I wondered if God was trying to say something, having us cross paths there at St. Catherine's. After staring at each other uncomfortably for a few moments, I broke the silence. "Charlie."

"Sean." The shock of seeing me eased into a look of concern. "I heard about the fallout from Bethesda. How are you holding up?"

I tried not to look surprised that she was as plugged in as she was; being the head of the local library tended to make her information central. It was more curious that she was going out of her way to talk to me. "I'm essentially on desk duty," I replied. "Until the Village Council considers my situation formally at its next meeting."

Charlie narrowed her eyes. "What's your read?"

I smiled wryly. "I've dusted off my resume, if that tells you anything."

"I see," she said thoughtfully.

"I put them into a bind," I said.

"Not an unusual situation for you as of late," she replied as she zipped up her jacket.

I blanched, knowing now the conversation had shifted. "That's not exactly fair," I said, my voice pitching up slightly. "In both cases I was doing my job."

Shaking her head at me, Charlie moved toward the door. "We're not doing this. Not here. *Especially* not here."

I snagged her by the arm, preventing her from making an escape. "If not now, when? We need to talk through this, Charlie."

Slipping out from my grasp, she shook her head again before pausing with one gloved hand on the ornate handle of the exit. "You need to find some clarity on that, Sean. When you do, *then* we can talk."

With a sudden swirl of snowflakes, she was gone, leaving me standing there quite alone in the vestibule of the sanctuary. I watched as the door gently swung shut on its pneumatic hinge but didn't really see it; instead, in my mind's eye, I replayed yet again those uncomfortable moments I'd spent grilling my own kin for a crime she had no part of.

The slight *chunk* when the door closed completely brought me back to the here and now, and I frowned before turning toward the sanctuary proper.

I knew the answers I sought couldn't be found in the ornate space, but hope sprung eternal nonetheless.

Four

Chase Cromwell looked like he was peacefully sleeping in the photo being displayed by my tablet –– save for the fact that the lower portion of his torso appeared to be hidden beneath the third row of a minivan. The color had, of course, long since drained from his face, much as his life had trickled away while officers had fruitlessly attempted to pinpoint the location from which his cell phone had dialed 9–1–1. What *was* visible of his torso appeared to be clad in logoed warmup, though I wasn't able to make out the mascot nor the words below it. The tennis racket he'd apparently been contorting himself to retrieve was a foot or so away from his blond hair, expensively cut and barely held back by a white head scarf bearing the same logo as the jacket.

After the initial shock of what I was seeing had passed, I'd turned the photo multiple times to try and make some sense out of the nearly impossible way his body had been crammed into the rear of the vehicle. I kept coming back to the strange twist in his body, and that tennis racket that seemed just out of reach; as many times as I'd been called to the scene of a death over the years, this one easily made my top ten list for strangest. I had to admit it the way it had been presented to me *seemed* plausible, if not amazingly dreadful.

My eyes focused for a moment on the racket. "Explain this to me again?" I asked.

The small mustachioed face in the lower corner of the video call nodded. "Kid is one of the stars of the high school tennis team and had the use of the family minivan to get to practice. From what we've been able to piece together, near as we can figure he pulled into the student parking lot; then, instead of popping the tailgate to get his gear for practice, he shimmied out of the driver's seat and tried to lean over the rear bench to retrieve his stuff. It's a typical teen stunt."

I looked at the picture again. "Except...?" I prompted.

"Yeah," the face grimaced. "The seat wasn't latched properly – the hooks had only partially engaged. As soon as Chase leaned over to grab his racket, the whole thing upended on top of him."

"Holy shit." I twisted the photo around yet again, my rational brain still unwilling to accept what I was seeing. "That has to have been a mil-lion–to–one chance of getting just the right angle to become trapped like that," I said softly, zooming in on the photo once again. "You really think he was trying to climb over the top? The body position is just so... *awkward*."

"Yeah. The nightmarish part is how the damn thing *locked* into its storage configuration – you know, the one where you get extra space for bulky items? Coroner confirmed it pinned him right at the diaphragm, too – and just far enough away from the controls, he wasn't able to reach the release button."

I nodded, more to ward off the intrinsic horror of what the detective at the other end of the call was relaying. "And it relentlessly squeezed him to death?"

"Yeah," the face nodded again. "He was a muscular kid for his age, due to being an athlete, so we figure he managed to fight the pressure for a bit. His phone was in the front seat, though; despite that, he man-aged to use the virtual assistant multiple times over the course of an hour to contact 9–1–1. I don't have to tell you, Sean, that cell phones make it nearly impossible for Dispatch to nail down a specific address."

"No kidding."

"The department managed to roll two cars – one after each call. Both drove through the damn lot, but neither saw anything suspicious and kept right on going."

"Who found him?"

"The father, about four hours later." He paused. "When his son didn't turn up for lunch, he pinged the kid's iPhone using that Find a Device feature."

"Jesus. No one missed him at practice?"

"No. It was an optional Saturday workout. Even though he normally attended, it wouldn't have been terribly unusual for him *not* to be there, either."

I looked at the photo again. "Mike, as tragic as this is, I've not heard anything suspicious yet. Why call me?"

The photo shrunk and visage of my old friend and prior mentor went full screen. "The case is more or less closed," Chief Michael Gilbert said. "By all accounts, it was a tragic accident. But the family is demanding an investigation *into* the investigation. Specifically, they want to know how it's possible not one, but *two* cars could have missed the minivan."

"Ah," I nodded. "Have they threatened a lawsuit?" I asked, feeling a bit of empathy for what Mike was going through; it wasn't dissimilar to the situation I was facing in Windeport.

"Not yet, Sean, but the subtext is clear. They feel as though we've dropped the ball. The coroner assures me the kid was likely dead by the time the second patrol rolled through, but there is a tiny chance the first one might have been able to save him, had they looked a bit harder. And that is where our exposure lies. I need to know, frankly, if we screwed up." He paused. "Or, at the very least, how big a check the City Council is gonna have to write."

"Internal investigations aren't my style," I demurred. "Are you sure you want me? There must be other people in your Rolodex, Mike."

"I need *you*, Sean. Someone from outside the department that I can trust to give me the straight answers I need."

"Mike——"

"Sean," he said in a low voice that caught me in mid-sentence. "Come out for a few days. Look over what we have and do what you do. Tell me what I think I already know so I can move forward." He squinted at me in the way I'd learned during endless hours on patrol to-gether revealed just how tired he was. "I realize it's a lot to ask, but I could really use a solid here. And if what the grapevine is saying about you back there in Windeport is accurate, it sounds like you might have the time, too."

Mike and I went back more years than I cared to admit; he was a decorated police officer, with multiple high–profile cases under his belt. He'd risen through the ranks far faster than I had, landing in his cur-rent Chief position after a celebrated career working homicide cases in Boston. I wasn't surprised word had reached him about me – we had multiple mutual friends in the business. Taking the rare action of call-ing in an outsider for such an investigation told me just how serious he thought the situation was, but it also served as a warning – a warning that the case was sticky enough he wanted no direct part in it. Bringing me in would help to blunt any fallout to his department, at the very real risk of damaging my own reputation in the process.

If I still have a reputation left to damage at this point, I thought to my-self.

I looked at the image of a teenager cut down before he'd truly started living and could feel the tug of a mystery that needed to be solved. Doug had managed to stave off the other members of the Council a sec-ond time, but he'd privately told me the third would be the charm; I couldn't deny not wanting to be in Windeport when the inevitable de-cision finally caught up with me. The purgatory I'd been experiencing – for weeks now – was preventing me from actually doing the job I'd been hired for in the first place.

I wondered if leaving town would spur them to action, and suddenly knew the answer.

"Send me what you have already, or give me access to your cloud share," I said to the small image of Mike. "I'll have my admin put to-gether a modified Mutual Aid Agreement and route it to you for a sig-nature." I laughed for reasons Mike wouldn't understand. "I won't wait for Windeport to cash your check before we see what flights from Port-land look like."

Mike smiled. "Southern California is nice this time of year," he replied brightly, as though a weight had been lifted from his shoulders. "I don't know if you still swim, but the beaches are magnificent."

I frowned. "Southern?" I asked, quickly checking the account he'd used to connect with me over FaceTime. I hadn't caught the fact that it was his personal email address, not an official departmental address; for some reason, that was triggering all sorts of alarm bells. "Mike... aren't you outside of Sacramento? Last I heard, they didn't have beaches."

"No," he laughed. "You need to keep up better on Linked In. I've been officially running the department down here in Rancho Linda for about a month now."

My expression froze. "Rancho Linda."

"Yeah," he said fondly. "It's just a bit south of Los Angeles and, as my kids remind me daily, less than ten miles from Disneyland. You'll love it."

"I'm sure I will," I said haltingly.

Mike caught something in my change in tone. "Sean? What's wrong?"

"I'm sorry," I smiled weakly. "Your change in posting just caught me by surprise. Look, let me get my act together and I'll get out there as soon as I can. Does that work?"

"Completely," Mike said, relief clear in his voice. "First round is on me when you touch down."

"I'm going to hold you to that," I said as I clicked off.

Waiting for a moment, I pushed back from my chair and stood behind the mid–century Modern desk that predated even the building my department was in and stepped over to the window that gave me a clear view of the athletic fields of the school behind the station. The snow was still a few feet deep, so the activity was admittedly sparse; I wasn't really seeing it, anyway, for in my mind's eye I was focused on another time entirely.

My iPhone sang out the jaunty tune that was the ringtone for Suzanne and broke my reverie. I pulled it from my pocket and smiled as I saw my girlfriend's photo on the lock screen before answering with video. "Milady," I said, falling into the nickname that had developed after a shared experience at Halloween the prior year. "How did you know I needed a friendly face?"

"Magic," she laughed. "I was going to head to *Millie's On The Wharf* for an early lunch. Are you game?" She smiled that smile that had a way of melting my heart on the spot. "It's all–you–can–eat shrimp, apparently. If I order, Millie can't stop me from sharing with my main squeeze. Even if I have to do it in the parking lot."

It had been a few weeks since my aunt had thawed enough to let me actually *stay* inside the restaurant instead of forcing me into takeout. "Absolutely," I said. "Say... when is that comic convention you wanted to go to?"

"The one in California?" she replied.

"Yeah."

"There are a few," she answered after a moment. "The big one in San Diego is July, but there's a smaller one in Anaheim coming up fairly quickly – like next week, if I'm not mistaken. Why?"

"Can you spare some time away from your practice?"

"Maybe," she said tentatively. "I can shuffle some stuff and get Doctor Nelson over in Lancaster to cover the rest. Why?"

I stared out across the snow and ice in the field behind my office, and knew it reflected how many felt about me in Windeport at the moment. "I think I've come up with a way for us to get there," I said, "and to be honest, I could use some time away from all of this."

"You'll be working?"

"Yeah, but I don't expect it to take long," I said, immediately knowing I was probably jinxing the enterprise entirely. "There should be plenty of time for us to cavort at the convention. If you can still get tickets, that is."

"I should," she laughed. "You just want to see me in costume again."

"I won't lie, it was the first thing I thought of," I lied, for it had been anything but.

Actually, Suze, I'm gonna need some serious moral support on this one, I thought, feeling slightly guilty that I was going to be leaning on her more than she knew.

"Liar," she laughed. "I'll call Yasmin and get back to you. When do we leave?"

"As soon as my admin can book the flights."

"Then I'd better hustle and get my bags packed."

I smiled as her image faded from the small screen, thankful again at how providence had brought the two of us together. With all of the other changes I'd been dealing with over the past few months, her love and support had been a constant I could steer my life by. Still thinking about Suzanne, I turned as my laptop chimed with incoming email; Mike hadn't wasted any time sending me the packet they'd created.

Sliding back into my chair, I picked up the desk phone and speed dialed my admin. "Caitlyn? Please tell me you're looking for something challenging to sink your teeth into...?"

Five

Caitlyn worked her usual magic and managed to book two seats on the first flight of the day out of the Portland International Jetport for the following morning. "Amazing as always," I said to her as she handed me the itinerary on my way past her reception desk in the foyer of the station. Pausing for a moment, I leaned against the semi–circular desk and smiled. "I'm not sure what I would do without you."

"I just know my way around the municipal travel system," she chuckled. "Sadly, your rental car is an economy off–brand of some sort. It's all that was left on such short notice." She smiled wider. "Fortunately for you, the Anaheim Marriott offers a Government Discount that rather amazingly falls *just* inside the per diem range."

"Does it now?" I smiled. "Good thing it's only a few miles from Rancho Linda."

"And mere steps from the Convention Center," she observed as she tried unsuccessfully to hide her smirk.

"I had no idea," I deadpanned as I slid the paperwork into my backpack.

"Your secret is safe with me, Chief," she winked. "But I'll keep it *longer* if you bring back a few autographs."

"From cartoon characters?" I frowned. "I haven't the first clue how to even do that. Is it even possible?"

"Dear Lord," Caitlyn laughed. "Suzanne has no idea what she's getting into, does she?" Seeing my panicked expression, she waved me away. "Don't worry, I'll text her my requests," she added, with a devilish smile. "I have faith *she* can come through for me."

"Good to know," I smiled weakly, wondering if I had somehow just been insulted. Leaning toward her, I lowered my voice and said conspiratorially: "Keep everything from imploding while I'm gone, would you? I know how everyone likes to slack off when I'm out of town."

"Absolutely, Chief," she laughed, enjoying the old joke. "See you when you get back."

The cramped sedan awaiting in the parking lot had been foisted upon me by our insurance carrier while we negotiated over what they would *actually* cover on the now bullet–ridden SUV; driving the short distance to my bungalow along the water was just about the limit of what I could stand. I was definitely not looking forward to taking it all the way to Portland. As I pulled out of the Public Safety Building's driveway and turned onto Route One, it occurred to me that winter made my small village of Windeport seem even more desolate than normal. Those who could afford to winter somewhere else had been gone since Thanksgiving; the rest of us were slogging through one of the worst seasons of the year, weathering snowstorm after snowstorm in an unending parade of cold misery that battered the psyche. The tri–tiered snowbanks along the narrowed Sea Road did a fairly good job of masking the battered clapboard houses I passed, as did the rows of empty lobster traps awaiting deployment in the spring.

Pulling into the driveway I'd shoveled by hand just that morning, I took in the mid–century Modern lines of the bungalow once more. I'd finally gotten over my father selling the century–old brick building that had housed the Colbeth Pharmacy for generations and the apartment above it that had been mine for years. While the eviction had stung – by family, no less – the pain had lessened immeasurably once I discovered Suzanne had become the new owner. She'd moved her practice into the former pharmacy space and taken over the apartment from me. In many ways it felt like I was getting the last laugh, though, for I generally spent several nights each week with her quite literally in my old bedroom.

The bungalow was another thing altogether. Not all that long ago, I'd been hunting for clues in that very carport to determine how the previous occupant had ended up dead in the back of his pickup truck. While I'd certainly made the place my own in the months since, I could never quite clear the sense that the spirit of Ingmar Pelletier hadn't completely moved on. I chalked it up to the New England superstitions that I'd been brought up on, including the great number of ghost stories along this part of the coast derived from lobstermen who'd never returned home. There was no question where Ingmar currently resided – or the person responsible for his death, for that matter – but that brought little comfort during the long, cold and sometimes lonely winter nights.

Lonely.

The thought resonated as I unlocked the door to the bungalow and dropped the keys into the dish on the counter. With Suzanne in my life, it was not something I by rights should be feeling, and yet, as I looked around the immaculate kitchen and the living room beyond, something was missing – and had been for a few months now. I wandered to the windows fronting the ocean and took a few moments to watch the waves crash over the rocky shoals out in the harbor, the chill of the afternoon easily felt through the thin glass. Sea smoke had begun to form thanks to the temperature inversion, lending the empty cove a more mysterious air than normal. It also served to cover the absence of normal activity, something I privately wished I could extend to other parts of my life.

I was used to packing efficiently, so it didn't take much time for me to pull together a few changes of clothing and a set or two of workout gear. After sliding out the suitcase from the closet, though, I paused at the costume Charlie had made for me to wear the prior Halloween. Running a finger along one of the details she had hand sewn, I was gutted once more at how our relationship had fractured, fallout from the Pelletier case. I'd tried to comfort myself with the notion that I'd been acting out of duty, which was certainly the core truth of the matter. Relatives, though, didn't forgive breaches of decorum as easily it seemed. Our recent chance encounter at St. Catherine's had me wondering, though, for she had hinted that repairs might just be possible.

Taking the costume down off its hanger, I carefully folded it into the suitcase, then nestled in the other parts beside it. I, for one, had grown tired of the situation, and as I slid the boots into the case she had hand dyed to match the costume, I impulsively decided enough was enough. Nothing was going to stop me from appearing on Charlie's doorstep upon my return from California; I just didn't seem to know how to start that conversation. Perhaps there was inspiration to find while in California, for continuing to avoid each other, given the small size of our village, was proving intolerable.

Zipping the suitcase closed, I ignored the *other* person that came to mind whenever I looked at the costume. That was a problem to be dealt with far sooner than I'd planned, it seemed.

Suzanne was waiting for me in the small parking lot at the rear of the old pharmacy building; after tossing her suitcase into the trunk of the sedan, she slid into the front seat and slid even further for a welcome kiss. The drive to Portland, and the hotel close to the airport where we were staying the evening, would take a few hours; longer with a stop for dinner about halfway. Fortunately, the weather was clear for the first time in days, though icy cold. Owing to the particular part of the calendar we were in, the early dusk immediately dropped into full-on inky black of night shortly after we got underway.

As I drove cross-country to reach the Interstate, we chatted about her day and other tidbits of town gossip she picked up as the lone family physician for miles in any direction. Only half of my mind was on the conversation, though, a point driven home to me as I turned up the onramp to head south to the big city.

"Did you want a full sit-down?" I asked as I came up to speed. "Or is McDonald's okay?"

Suzanne chuckled. "Now I know for *sure* you've been ignoring me for the last ninety minutes."

That made me turn. "I'm not ignoring you," I said defensively.

"Right," she laughed deeper. "Then we might need to have a neurological exam once you get back from California, for we had this very conversation not twenty minutes ago."

I could feel a slight warming to my face. "Ah," I replied as I shifted lanes to pass a semi carrying a load of wood. "IHOP it is," I laughed. "Sorry."

Suze put a hand to my arm. "What's got you so introspective?" she asked. "I've never seen you like this before. Is it this case you're on?"

"Mostly," I replied.

"Tell me."

I sighed, wondering if I could reveal to her everything that was bothering me about the trip to California. The view from my living room window popped into my head, and I blinked to refocus on the road and the conversation. "Mike Gilbert is an old friend," I started. "He was my superior when I first became an officer, but his star was on the rise at the time and he only stayed in Maine for a few years. He's smart," I added. "I've never seen anyone take in a crime scene quite the way he can."

"How did he get to California?"

"By way of Boston," I answered. "He solved a number of high–profile cases and was recruited away by some county in Northern California. That's where I thought he was, actually. It caught me a bit off guard that he was closer to Los Angeles."

I could see her nodding slightly. "Your career that could have been?" she asked softly. "Is that what this is?"

Suzanne was perceptive, but I shook my head. "No, not at all. I made a conscious choice to stay in Maine; Mike wanted to get as far away as he could. We're both happy with our paths in this field, I think." I randomly checked the gauges for the umpteenth time and dryly noted to myself that there was still three–quarters of a tank of gas left.

"He's also quite the political animal. Calling me in is pretty shrewd, for if I uncover anything that reflects poorly on the department, it'll be from an outsider." I paused. "And if I don't find anything, I'll be on the next plane out and just as quickly forgotten."

"Why on earth would you take a case like that?" Suzanne asked, her voice vibrating with disdain. "And if he's any kind of friend of yours, how could he even dream of putting you in such a position? This is nuts!"

"I know," I sighed. "But he's a friend. And, to be honest, I need some time away."

Suzanne crossed her arms and sat back in her seat. "This isn't like you," she said. "Taking the first opportunity to escape your troubles."

"I'm tired," I replied. "Tired of the constant negative feedback loop I seem to be in. Tired of being treated like I'm an outsider when I'm anything but."

"Outsider? In *Windeport*?" she asked incredulously. "You've lived there your whole life!"

"True," I nodded. "But times change; personal ancestry won't help me this round. The village is going through a rough patch and I'm the most visible target." I sighed. "And I've been off my game as of late. It's been noticed."

"I will never understand the small-town mentality. Correct me if I'm wrong, but you did solve a *major crime*, right?"

"Last time I checked," I laughed ruefully. Deciding a change in topic was in order, I shifted the conversation to more mundane matters. "Do you remember if there is an IHOP in Augusta?"

"Right off the Interstate," she replied. Out of the corner of my eye, I could see she had the *we'll pick this up later* look.

"Good," I said as I changed lanes again and prepared to exit. "Because I could really use some chocolate chip pancakes tonight."

Six

Perhaps as an omen of things to come, while we managed to get out of Portland on time the following morning, our connection in Chicago was delayed six hours – first by weather, then by needing a crew replacement as a result of the weather delay. While I couldn't argue with wanting a well–rested Captain at the helm, by the time we touched down in Los Angeles a bit after six in the evening local time, I gained a very dim view of the airline industry writ large. Man (or women) does not subsist on peanuts and free soda alone, but despite my stomach telling me it was much later than what the digital clocks of Terminal One would have me believe, I knew food would have to wait just a bit longer.

Suzanne seemed to sense my foul mood and, as only she could, made me feel better just by looping her arm inside mine and leaning her head against my shoulder as we made our way to baggage claim. It was such a small gesture and yet such a meaningful one, bespeaking the care and support she had relentlessly offered me since becoming a couple last fall. Despite all of the uncertainties ahead, having her by my side went a long way toward decreasing my blood pressure.

LAX was several magnitudes of order larger than Portland, of course, as the bustling diverse crowd reminded me; it wasn't my first time on the West Coast, though. For whatever reason, riding the down escalator chose that moment to be the melancholy reminder of the last time I'd been out several years earlier. Deidre had insisted on signing us up for a 10K race at the Disneyland Resort, apparently something that had been on her bucket list. The very thought of going to a theme park had turned me off but I'd been a dutiful boyfriend and had accompanied her to the event. We'd stepped onto that very escalator and with no small amount of irony, Deidre had caught the tread just wrong and twisted her ankle badly enough that walking – let alone running – wound up being out of the question.

Then as now, the airport seemed to be perennially under construction. By the time we located the correct carousel, our bags were already slowly moving about the aluminum belt. "Guess I didn't need to offer up that prayer of contrition after all," I said to Suzanne as I grabbed our bags one after the other.

"I didn't peg you as the religious sort," Suzanne replied.

"I'm not particularly," I said. "It's actually a line from a favorite song I've not heard in a while." I sighed as I watched the throngs heading in the same general direction as we needed to go in order to retrieve our rental. "Once more unto the breach, Milady," I said.

"I've not been to Los Angeles in ages," Suzanne said nonchalantly as she again looped her arm inside of mine. "Most of the medical conferences I attend are usually in Orlando, but there was one here about seven years ago." She laughed. "All I remember is being stuck in traffic, no matter where I wanted to go. Six lanes of it. San Diego seems only marginally better, but then again, I've only been there during Comic–Con."

Recognizing she was trying to draw out of me why I was so dour, I smiled and pointedly ignored her invitation to reminisce. "I don't think that has changed much," I groaned good naturedly as we passed through the open door to the curb for arrivals. A blast of exhaust and blaring horns assaulted my senses. "And we still have – at best – a half–hour drive ahead of us."

"You *have* been here before, then?" Suzanne pounced at the infinitesimal opening I'd provided, masking it with a smile.

So much for avoiding that conversation, I thought. "Yes," I sighed, bowing to the inevitable.

"I'm getting the distinct impression it wasn't a fun outing."

"No, it wasn't," I acknowledged as we pressed through the crowd on the sidewalk and crossed to the island where the rental car busses were designated to retrieve us. Sandwiched between unpredictable streams of traffic as it was, the cacophony in the arrivals area thankfully precluded any further conversation for the moment; it wasn't until we were staring at the two–door caricature of a car deemed to be my rental that Suzanne spoke again.

"It'll be easy to park," she laughed as I popped open the hatchback and tried to wrestle our luggage into the trunk.

"This must be Caitlyn's idea of a joke," I apologized. "She said there wasn't much available, but to be honest I expected to be saddled with a minivan. Or one of those massive sedans favored by grandmothers in Palm Springs."

"She doesn't strike me as the type to pull a practical joke on her boss," Suzanne observed.

"I suppose... not..." I said through gritted teeth; my blood pressure rising with each shift of the luggage I made until I was finally able to slam the hatchback shut. If this *was* a joke, I'd was going to need to have a long chat with my admin when I got back.

Ten minutes later, after managing to not get us killed in my escape from the LAX rental area, I picked up our conversation thread. "To answer your question, I was out here with Deidre a number of years ago; we'd travelled a few places together for vacation, but that particular year she had it in her mind to run one of those special themed events that Disney hosted at their parks."

"I've seen them," Suzanne said. "I thought they were only in Orlando, though?"

"Not back then –– hey, is that my turn off for the 605 coming up?" I interrupted.

Suzanne checked her iPhone. "Next exit."

"Thanks," I said as I started to work my way across the rush hour traffic. "This reminds me of why I never moved to Boston." Changing lanes one more time, I continued. "It's been years now, but Disney used to host races on both coasts. They even had some special two–for–one deals where you could run here at the beginning of the week, and take in a race at the parks in Orlando at the end of the same week."

"That's crazy!"

"I know, right?" I laughed, my mood tempering finally. "I'm not a huge fan of crowds or overpriced attractions, but she was determined to do it. De wore me down enough that I agreed to come with her."

"I didn't realize you ran those things."

"I don't – I came purely to cheer her on. I'm a swimmer and have no plans to change sports any time soon. I do some land training of course, maybe twenty miles a week now. If that. Certainly not a half–marathon, though."

"How did she do?" Suzanne asked. "And your exit is coming up pretty fast."

"Thanks," I replied as I swerved to avoid a motorcycle that had crept into my blind side. "Not well. She twisted her ankle at the airport and wound up spending the entire weekend in our hotel room."

"Didn't she get it looked at? I can't believe you came all the way out here and didn't at least see the sights."

"Oh, we went to an urgent care where she got it wrapped up, and I picked up a bottle of ibuprofen and some crutches at a pharmacy close to Disneyland. But she'd had her heart set on the race. No race meant no fun. For either of us."

"Look for the 91," Suzanne said. "If I read this right, it will come up fast."

"Got it," I said.

For whatever reason, weaving through nasty Los Angeles traffic, I found myself in an introspective mood. "I've never thought about it un-til now, Suze, but that was a microcosm of our relationship. We tended to move in a direction that suited Diedre; as I look back, there were very few times when we shared an activity that we *both* liked."

"Or did something that you had wanted to do?" Suzanne said softly. "How often did she attend a Master's Swim Meet?"

I blinked. "Never," I said slowly.

"Exit! Exit! Exit!" Suzanne said urgently.

"Sorry!" I cried over my shoulder as I used a patented police move to swerve between two vehicles; I hit the clover leaf–shaped exit a bit faster than was reasonable, forcing both of us into our seats. Somehow, there was a slim spot available to insert our vehicle into the traffic and I barreled directly into it, braking hard to avoid smashing into the tailgate of a truck.

"We're here for a bit," Suzanne said. It wasn't lost on me that she'd braced her hand against the ceiling. "Look, you don't have to answer this if you don't want to, but... you dated her for close to ten years. Were you *planning* on marrying her at some point? Or was yours more of the 'don't need paper to make our love real' type of relationship?"

It wasn't exactly an unexpected question. Suzanne had appeared on the scene just as Deidre quite literally vanished from my life; I'd spent a number of sleepless nights re–litigating all of the arguments I'd made to myself that late fall afternoon at Quincy Market. "There was a time when I thought we'd get married," I said honestly. "After our first year together, I decided she was the one and treated her to a long weekend in Portland. I showed her the ring over dinner at DiMillo's, and she smiled and told me she wasn't quite ready to commit."

"Fancy place to get burned," Suzanne said. I could hear a trace of snark in her voice.

"I figured she just needed some time to get her feet under her."

"Right."

"No, seriously – her parents had dumped the grocery store on her right after she graduated from the University, decamping to Florida as most retirees seem to do. Those first few years were a bit rough, but she turned it around in the end."

"Did you ask again?"

"Several times. And I got variations on the same theme; after my fourth flame–out, I put the ring back into the safe deposit box and assumed she wanted to stay in the 'going–steady' part of the ledger." I sighed. "And I was happy with it. We had a good thing going, until I apparently ruined it."

"How on earth could you have ruined it?" Suzanne said. "And your turn is in less than three miles."

"Thanks." I sped up a bit to get around a line of slower vehicles. "Two mistakes, I think. After my mother died, I kind of threw myself into my career and took Deidre for granted; in retrospect, I think her attempts to pull me out of the cocoon I'd spun around me was her subtle way of telling me she was *finally* ready to get married, but I managed to successfully ignore her signals." I smiled mirthlessly. "As patient as she could be, even Deidre had limits; I'm certain now that was the beginning of the end."

Traffic suddenly took off, and I spent a moment carefully coming up to speed before continuing. "The final death knell was not wanting children, Suze," I explained. "Although I *thought* she felt the same way. Turns out, she didn't." I paused. "Look," I started, glancing at her. "We've not been dating long enough to have discussed this yet... and this is probably the worst time for you to find that out about me—"

Suzanne chuckled. "You mistake me for mother material, kitty," she said, using the nickname borne from our shared experience the prior Halloween. "I may love all things anime, but I have zero desire to raise any heathen of my own." She laughed again. "I will have to work with you on the Disney angle, though. Clearly you've never gone with a theme park veteran."

"I didn't know you'd been, or were a fan." I could sense she was tactfully shifting the topic, aware perhaps, that Deidre was still a sensitive subject.

"It was my parent's fault, actually. Dad grew up watching re-runs of *The Wonderful World of Disney* and somehow managed to get us to Orlando every year for Christmas. Talk about crowds! It was insane, but those trips are also some of my most cherished, magical memories."

"A theme park?" I asked skeptically. "It's all make-believe fantasy layered upon very ordinary midway attractions."

"Well, when you say it like *that*," she chuckled. "Don't worry, I wouldn't dream of forcing you. Change your mind, though, and I'm your Guest Relations cast member."

"Guest Rela——"

"Turn now, kitty!"

I pushed my way through traffic and exited one freeway for another. Traffic was more intense on the final stretch, causing our conversation to fall into a lull as I attempted to navigate the mess without clipping anyone. It wasn't until I pulled up beneath the awning of the Marriott's entrance that I realized my knuckles were white from gripping the wheel.

"That was fun," I said as I put the car into park and leaned over to kiss Suzanne. "Sorry. I'm not comfortable with that many lanes of traffic going."

"No worries," she laughed. "It was the best E–ticket I've had yet."

Seven

Late cocktails, a later dinner and some beneficial bedroom calisthenics improved my outlook on life immeasurably; waking up next to Suzanne was a pleasurable experience under any circumstance, and as I watched her slowly begin to stir, it dawned on me this could qualify as our first official long–distance trip together. We'd spent a handful of three–day weekends in various bed–and–breakfasts across New England, and the occasional holiday in Boston; nothing, though, that required travel by plane. I decided I wanted to do more, at least as much as the demands of our mutual careers would allow.

Looking back on it, I realized I'd never had those thoughts with Deidre.

I rather reluctantly left Suzanne at the hotel after joining her for breakfast at the elegant (if not rather outrageously expensive) buffet on offer. Although she'd been able to procure tickets to the convention for the two of us, Suzanne had to appear in person at Will Call to obtain them. Given how many hero–themed folks were milling around the lobby of the hotel that morning, she'd observed that getting there early might be a wise idea – despite the fact the convention didn't start until the following evening. After she extracted a promise that I would return in time for lunch, I kissed her farewell and subjected myself yet again to rush hour traffic to connect with Mike.

Rancho Linda was northeast of Anaheim, as the crow flies. Getting to it, however, was anything *but* a straight line; my iPhone had dutifully given me multiple routes to the coffee shop Mike had recommended, but none were less than thirty minutes. I tried not to grimace as I snaked my way through housing developments and strip malls, at times driving with and then against prevailing commuter currents.

Southern California represented this weird snapshot of a time capsule to me. Here and there were cute single–family bungalows that evoked the residential boom that occurred just after the Second World War; those were dwarfed by more "modern" tract housing from the late sixties and early seventies, most of which had not withstood the test of time and were looking rather long in the tooth. Then, out of nowhere, a brilliant specimen from the Googie era would appear, all round lines with smooth arches and space–age colors. The whiplash such clashing architectural styles produced appeared to be something the residents took in stride. It was jarring enough that I found myself yearning for the classic lines and peeling clapboards of Windeport.

I passed smart looking libraries and classic town squares that I'd probably seen in a movie or two, reminding me that the film industry tended to stay close to home whenever possible – but could also make a random side street in Placentia look like some neighborhood outside of Boston. As I drove past one municipal park, I found myself recalling when a remake of a classic film was shot on location in Portland back when I was in high school. It had been apparently cheaper to use movie magic to make key areas there look like Philadelphia than to have *actually* filmed in Pennsylvania. I couldn't recall if the movie had been successful or not, but knew that friends of mine who'd grown up in Portland were still irate at the sleight of hand. I wondered what it meant that a whole city could stand in for another, temporarily, hiding its true self from the world for a brief instant in time.

California felt very much to me like it was *constantly* burying its true nature from the world in general. I'd not watched much television growing up – the demands of Olympic training tended not to allow for downtime – but what I *had* caught were programs centered in and around Los Angeles – mostly cop shows, of course – and they'd presented such a sanitized version of the area that I nearly didn't recognize it when I finally did visit. Not hiding, perhaps; maybe, in a sense, it had yet to discover what it was and how to show its true self to the world. Given how it had been hidden for so long, I wondered if California could even remember what it had once wanted to be.

The unusual duality the state represented intrigued me, though I wasn't entirely sure why.

I managed to only be five minutes late pulling into the coffee shop. Almost as if to underscore my earlier train of thought, it was a perfectly preserved Googie structure, with an oddly angled sign above a fly–away roofline and floor–to–ceiling windows exposing the diners to the cars passing on the street. As I locked the car, I could see where the neon lights would accent the structure after dark, and nodded slowly at the overall effect. Grudgingly, I had to admit that it was a beautiful example from a time that no longer existed.

Mike flagged me down as I entered the dining room, and I slid into the semi–circular booth after giving him a hearty hand-shake–slash–manly hug. His hair had more grey to it than the video call had displayed, and in person, I could see he'd put on quite a bit of weight. Fine lines had appeared at the edges of his eyes when he'd grinned at my appearance, and though he outwardly seemed ebullient, I quickly noticed the undercurrent of tension.

I made a tick mark in my mental ledger; I'd already guessed his desire to meet at the diner instead of his station house had been calculated to enable him to speak without the walls hearing his conversation with me. My sense of unease about the undertaking grew a bit stronger, but a promise was a promise.

"Mike, you've gotten old," I said good naturedly as the waitress took my order for coffee. "And this is not the first round I was expecting."

"You were late," he chuckled, a deep–throated affair that I used to find would bring a smile to the sourest of expressions. "And *you* look like you're still training for the Olympics."

"Who says I'm not?" I smiled as my eyes flicked down to his break-fast. "You look like you're eating as if you *were* still training," I said, look-ing back up.

He frowned a bit and played with the stack of flapjacks still on his plate. I knew I wasn't that late, but the syrup had already congealed around the sausage at the edge. "I wish," he said softly. "Eating is one thing I've done a lot more of since taking this gig in Rancho Linda."

"Comes with the job; any chief would tell you that," I replied as a steaming mug of coffee appeared at my elbow, along with the requisite container of sugar. "And you worked in Boston! I'd assume any posting after *that* would be a piece of cake."

"You would," he nodded. "Funny, that's what Julie said when this opening popped up."

"How's that wife of yours?" I asked. I'd only met her at the wedding, and that was many years earlier, when they'd still been living in Boston; my impression of her was formed fully by the holiday cards she dutifully sent me each year. Though I'd watched Mike's kids grow over a succession of holidays, they could well have been Photoshopped in from clipart as well as I knew them.

I wondered if my definition of "friendship" needed to be adjusted, given how little I actually knew about Mike and his family.

"Good," he said as he sliced a hunk from the side of the stack of flapjacks and shoveled it into his mouth. After munching for a moment, he added: "They promoted her out of the classroom and into a vice–principal role. It's not exactly what she wanted to do, but the money is good, and she doesn't have to grade papers on the weekend any longer."

"Ah, victim of her own success?"

"Something like that," he said. "How's Deidre?"

"Don't have a clue," I said easily. "We broke up last fall, and she moved to Georgia."

"Georgia?" he asked, eyes wide. "After all those years together... that seems... sudden."

"It was for one of us," I nodded. "In the end, though, I think it was for the best."

"Right," Mike said, though from his expression I could tell he had a million more questions he wanted to ask. My own must have told him not to push his luck, for he returned to devouring his breakfast.

Sipping my coffee, I let the silence grow between us for a bit. It was an old interrogation trick, one that I was reasonably certain wouldn't work on Mike. Surprisingly, though, once it became uncomfortable, he started to speak. "The family's lawyer notified the Town Council late yesterday they intend to file a Wrongful Death lawsuit against Rancho Linda. While I wasn't privy to the actual conversation, the amount they are demanding was enough that my boss – the Town Manager – apparently went white with shock."

"Damn."

"Yeah." He held his fork out. "Look, I think my guys messed up. Badly."

I frowned. "That's not quite the impression you gave me the other day, Mike."

"I know, and I'm sorry about that," he replied as he sipped what looked like a Coke from a green–tinted and oddly curved glass. I'd seen loggers in northern Maine prefer that as their morning caffeine hit over coffee, and idly wondered if Mike still kept a stash under his desk. "Until yesterday, I didn't want to believe we had any exposure. But the lawsuit has everyone rattled."

"Enough that you are rethinking everything?" I replied, eyebrows raised. "Why?"

"The first car called to the scene – within about ten minutes of the initial 9–1–1 call – was an unmarked with two of my best detectives. They'd caught another case in the area, but since they were the closest vehicle to the call, dispatch diverted them."

"Hang on, Mike. That wasn't the point of my question, and I'm not sure you should be telling me this. You have to let me do my own discovery."

"You need some context, Sean. Context that is not in the files. Context that will let you ask the *right* questions."

"All right," I said slowly.

"I've been considering splitting that pair for a few weeks now––"

My eyes widened. "The detectives? Why?"

Mike shrugged. "Personality clash, primarily. To be honest, as good as they are those two are opposites in more ways than I can count." He paused again. "Now I'm thinking it could be at the root of our problem, for there was a disagreement between them regarding how much effort to expend in locating what one of them thought was a phantom call."

"Shit."

"Exactly. There's no documentation of this of course, I only have the statement from one of the detectives to that effect; the other simply doesn't recall any sort of conversation."

I slurped my coffee, a knot forming in my stomach. "This would have been nice to have known before flying out here, Mike. You've put me into the middle of a mess, haven't you?"

"Don't thank me yet," he laughed grimly. "It gets worse. The second car was another detective – one that I recently demoted and has an axe to grind. Even though he also failed to find the missing kid, he wound up as the lead investigator on the case and has been a royal pain in my ass ever since."

"Why?"

"When he couldn't immediately locate the kid, he protested being pulled off for another call that was deemed more urgent. He disagreed vehemently with Dispatch – it's on tape, unfortunately – and that tape has wound up in the hands of the family. I think he's the one who leaked it with the intimation that the department did something wrong," he said. "I can't prove it. But I need you to find out so I can end his sorry career once and for all."

I nodded. "Even if it *was* a breach of protocol, Mike, I can't guarantee I won't uncover what he's alleging."

"You won't," Mike said. "It was an unfortunate circumstance – a once in a lifetime set of unusual events that we'd never be able to replicate in a million years."

"Are you talking about the seat? Or the movements of your personnel?"

"Both, I suppose," he said as he tossed his fork to the plate, the unfinished stack of flapjacks ignored as he wiped his mustache with a napkin. "The thing is, I know I can trust you to find out what happened, Sean.

I want to believe we had no part in the kid's death, but if we did, we need to accept responsibility for it – for whatever comfort that brings the family. And if it also means I can eliminate a few bad apples from the department as well," he smiled wryly, "so much the better."

I toyed with the ceramic mug in my hands, idly noting it, like the rest of the surroundings in the coffee shop, was period perfect. "You know how I work, Mike. I will follow the trail wherever it leads. It might mean having to answer tough questions." I looked up at him. "I've known you for a long time and value our friendship. If recent events are any indicator, this could damage that irrevocably. Are you certain you want *me* to look into this?"

"Yes," Mike said without hesitation. "I need *you*. Not some lacky from the County's Internal Affairs department that would bury any wrongdoing in a report that never gets published. I trust you." He looked out the window before adding, "Even if that means you find something that forces me to resign."

"If it comes to that?" I asked, still uncertain that I might not be the ultimate fall guy if the investigation went south.

"Yes," he repeated after turning and catching my eye. "I hope it won't."

Something had changed my friend. Where once my mentor had seemed clear eyed about right and wrong, this strange need to protect his department's reputation was out of character. Part of me wanted to chalk it up to the horrific death they were dealing with and the unusual chain of events around it. As I looked at Mike, I wondered for the first time if playing the game for as long as he had might not have finally caught up with him.

I waited a long moment before nodding. "All right."

"Good." He slid out of the booth and I followed behind him. As we waited to pay the check at the host stand, his phone buzzed with a text message, which he read before turning toward me. "I've asked the lead investigator to meet us here so he can walk you through the original material. Though it's not my first choice, I've assigned him to also act as your aide while you're working the case," he said. "They'll be able to get you anything you need from the department."

"I don't need a minder," I said, arching an eyebrow. "And isn't that the detective you think leaked to the family?"

"Yes, and you'll be minding *him*," Mike replied. "I need to keep him on a tight leash. But you'll need access, so he's been deputized to get you anything without needing to seek my approval." He laughed a bit more. "Which is ironic, now that I think about it."

"Why?"

"I may have demoted him, but he's still a damn fine investigator. If he plays his cards right, I won't be able to touch him after the dust settles." Mike waved his debit card in my face. "Having him joined with you at the hip will help you find me proof of what he did. And prevent him from doing it again."

I shook my head. "This is a tangled mess, Mike."

"Isn't it, though?" he chuckled.

"Thanks for breakfast," I added as we headed out to the parking lot.

"I still owe you a drink," he laughed. "We can catch it this evening after you've gotten your feet beneath you."

"Sounds like a deal," I said.

Mike's smile faltered as he looked over my shoulder. "Ah, here's your temporary partner now," he said. "Sean, I'd like to introduce you to Detective Junior Grade Korsokovach."

Eight

"Detective," I said as I extended my hand. Leaning against an unmarked SUV, Vasily was dressed impeccably in a button–down open at the collar and carefully color coordinated khakis. His hair was still long and pulled back into the ponytail he'd worn while working with me, but his blond coloring seemed lighter than I remembered. There was also a shadow of a beard along the chiseled lines of his face, something that appeared to be in fashion these days. After a lifetime of friendship, not to mention a decade of being partners, I immediately caught the look he flashed me as he straightened up to reach for my hand.

"A pleasure to meet you...?" he smiled as we shook, his carefully schooled face betraying absolutely no recognition.

"Sean Colbeth," I said, quickly deciding to play along. In an instant I realized Mike had no idea of our connection, which was odd; even a quick look at Vasily's service jacket would have prominently listed his status as my de facto number two for nearly a decade. For an officer he was bent on cashing out of the department, it was surprising he was so uninformed.

It was another non sequitur, adding to my overall discomfort around the situation.

"Sean is Chief of the Windeport Police Department. He's the investigator I told you I was bringing in," Mike explained.

"Windeport?" Vasily repeated, giving me a quizzical expression.

"A small, out of the way seaside village in Maine," I chuckled, impressed at his acting abilities. I had to lean into my interrogator skills not to betray anything myself. "I'm not surprised you've never heard of it."

"I'll wager the seafood is good," he smiled.

"It is."

"I've got to get back to the station, Sean," Mike said after a quick glance at his phone. "Vasily will take you from here. If you want to grab that drink tonight, we can compare notes after you've had a chance to settle in."

"Sounds good," I replied as I shook his hand and watched him depart in a late model unmarked sedan. Once I was sure he'd driven out of sight, I whirled on Vasily. "What the Hell have I gotten into?" I asked. "And what's with the charade?"

Vasily glanced upward and I followed, noting the security cameras outside of the coffee shop. "Not here," he said quietly. "Do you have a vehicle?"

"Yeah, that sorry excuse over there," I answered, pointing to my rental.

His eyes widened. "That can't be very comfortable at all."

"My head hits the roof, and I can't get the seat back far enough. But it will do."

"You can't leave it here," he said thoughtfully. "Why don't you follow me to the station? Then we can head out to the school so you can see the scene of the crime."

"Crime?" I repeated. "I admit I've only gotten tidbits at this point, but *crime* doesn't seem to fit what I've been told so far."

Vasily looked grim. "We'll see how you feel after we go through everything, Chief."

The station turned out to be just a few blocks from the coffee shop, and Vasily badged me into the private lot around the rear of the two-story brick building. I was surprised at how big the station was, but then again, everything in California had a propensity for being larger than it needed to be. Grabbing my backpack out of the rear of the rental, I locked up and slid into the passenger seat of Vasily's SUV.

I couldn't ignore the turbulent emotions that were roiling inside my stomach from the unexpected appearance of my best friend. Maybe *unexpected* wasn't quite right; anticipated was more appropriate, I supposed, given I'd known Rancho Linda had been the posting he'd gone to so he could be closer to his family. Part of me had hoped to have a chance to connect with him socially, but since neither of us had spoken since that day at Maine Medical Center, I'd not mustered up enough courage to text him.

What I hadn't counted on was getting thrown together with him. The first ten things I wanted to say to Vasily as he put the SUV into drive and pulled out of the lot died on my lips; the eleventh was, even to my ears, admittedly lame.

"You never returned my phone calls."

"No," he replied smoothly. "I was serious about wanting to get away from you and everything you represented. Talking to you again would have only made it worse."

"Of course," I said, nodding as if I could comprehend.

But I couldn't.

As I sat there watching the palm trees go by it became crystal clear to me just how much his departure had cost me personally. Vasily had always been there as a friend and confidant; we were complementary halves of a whole that had been ripped asunder. Having Suzanne in my life had soothed some of the emotional pain, to be sure. Whatever peace I had made with it, though, was threatening to crumble. "You want to explain why you didn't tell your Chief you knew me?"

He smiled as we turned a corner. "I'm already on thin ice as it is. If he had known about us, he'd have assigned someone else to nursemaid you and the case into oblivion."

I raised my eyebrows in surprise. "How is it he hasn't read your jacket?"

"He's only been here *officially* for a month," Vasily replied. "The prior Chief left him with a few fires, and with the deputy position is still open, he's a bit shorthanded. Given how many officers are under his purview, I'm not sure he's even had the time to review his senior staff fully."

"This isn't ethical," I reminded him. "You're one of the detectives I'm supposed to be reviewing!"

"I'm not worried," he laughed. "If anyone can be counted on to be fair and equitable, it would be you, Sean. No matter the circumstance."

I chuckled bleakly. "Tell that to Windeport."

Vasily turned toward me as he pulled to a stop at an intersection. "What do you mean by that?"

"Let's just say I've become a bit of a pariah back home," I said wearily. "You were the smart one, I think. Getting out, getting away."

"Small town mentality," he said softly. "I get it."

"Why the demotion?" I asked.

Vasily grimaced. "I'd prefer not to get into that."

"You can't have it both ways, Vas. You want me to help? I need to know everything."

He drove for a few blocks in silence, but the rising color on his face nearly told me everything on its own. "The short version," he started, "is that I slept with my partner."

"Jesus, Vasily!" I breathed. "You didn't waste much time."

His face flamed further. "Spare me your sanctimoniousness," he snapped. "You're not the one that left his career and the object of his desire behind in an attempt to start over cleanly! I arrived in California with no friends and no life to speak of." He took a deep breath. "And as it turns out, I landed in the one part of the state that remains rather closed to alternative lifestyles such as mine."

The vehemence in his voice startled me. This was not the carefree yet emotional soul I'd said goodbye to months ago; no, his time in California had given him an edge that was uncomfortable to see. With a shock, I realized *both* of us appeared to have been affected as byproduct of his departure, though I was pretty sure the scope of those changes was just becoming clear. "Vasily..."

"It was my own fault," he continued, waving me off. "I knew better, of course. You'd trained me well enough," he chuckled wryly. "But I thought I could handle it. Until the day he accused me of harassment."

"Shit."

"Yeah," he sighed. "Turns out, I was in the way of his upward mobility. Once I was sidelined by the accusation – and the demotion that came with it, ultimately – his chances improved immeasurably for the coveted senior spot we were both up for."

My stomach flipped. "Please... *please* tell me he wasn't in the other car...?"

He smiled again, a bit ruefully. "Very little gets past you, Chief."

Nine

As used to New England architecture as I was, the low-slung buildings comprising the Rancho Linda High School looked more like some sort of bucolic office campus than an institution of learning. Vasily had been able to drive around two sides of the school owing to how the streets were laid out, pointing out to me the major highlights before turning into a long driveway that wound its way down a slight slope to the vast student parking lot. Hundreds of cars were there, which was unsurprising given that it was a school day.

Slowing the SUV, Vasily pointed up the hill behind the lot. "School is about four hundred feet that way," he said, "though you'd never know it given the bushes and undergrowth. The athletic fields are three hundred feet down the other path."

I put a hand up against the late morning sun. "So effectively, the lot is hidden from both the school and the fields?"

"Much to the delight of the smokers," Vasily laughed. "Here's the parking spot where the van was ultimately found," he said as he stopped in the middle of an aisle and put the SUV into park.

"It's fairly close to either pathway," I said. "I assume the lot was much emptier on the weekend."

"Not as much as you would think," Vasily frowned. "That's partly what made it such a mess. There were multiple activities going on at the school that weekend," he continued as he pulled out his notebook and flipped a few pages. "Three sports aside from tennis had practice, and there was a swim meet at the pool. A science fair was also in progress in the auditorium and the PTA was hosting a charity lunch in the cafeteria."

"Damn. And no one saw anything?"

"Hard to say," Vasily replied. "By the time we managed to get an actual investigation going, everything had pretty much ended for the day and the school was empty."

That made me pause. "But you knew what was going on that day," I pointed out. "You could——"

"Yeah, we didn't do any of that," Vasily said grimly. "Once the coroner ruled it was an accident, any appetite for doing due diligence went out the window. And with the family breathing down the Chief's neck, he wanted this case closed out quickly."

I pushed out of the SUV and stood in front of the parking spot. There wasn't anything immediately notable about it save for the fact it was remarkably unoccupied in an otherwise full area. Slowly turning to take in the rest of the lot, I smiled a bit at the wide variation in late-model vehicles crammed into every square foot; while it wasn't a uniquely Californian teenage rite of passage to be stuck driving around the family clunker, the sheer magnitude of vehicles certainly was, underscoring the state's ongoing love affair for the automobile. About the only thing tying the discordant mix of models together was a uniquely shaped parking sticker with pride of place upon each front windshield.

Turning back to the spot where Chase's minivan had been found, it was easy to see the lines were faded and the asphalt cracked, signs that the school wasn't entirely keeping up with facilities maintenance. A small makeshift shrine of sorts was propped up against the concrete barrier, though, and I pulled out my iPhone to snap a few shots. It wasn't much – only a cross wrapped in dying flowers and a few photos of Chase from better days – but it felt significant that someone had thought to pull one together.

"How long has this been here?" I asked as I knelt to get a few close–up shots.

"It popped up a day or two after the kid was found. School tells me the other students have been avoiding using this spot, turning it into a de facto memorial."

I looked up at Vasily. "What kind of kid was Chase?" I asked.

Vasily chuckled.

"What?" I asked, perplexed.

"I've missed you," he said simply. "No one here investigates like you do."

I stood up. "Knowing the victim––"

"Exactly," he nodded. "It's the first step toward understanding what happened. No one here seems to get that."

My mouth quirked. "Maybe it's a Maine thing," I offered. "California *is* kind of weird."

He sighed. "Even growing up here, I still don't get the culture. Nor understand it at times." He flipped his notebook pages once more. "Chase was a straight–A student, varsity letter winner in tennis. Berkeley already hooked him with a full ride after graduation. Well–liked by teachers, based on the few interviews I was able to conduct before Chief Gilbert pulled the plug. Aside from the parents, I didn't talk to anyone else."

"Not even other students?"

"No."

"Tell me about the minivan," I asked as I circled the spot, snapping photos. The hilliness of the area surprised me; for some reason I'd assumed it was fairly flat in that part of the state. Squinting, off in the distance I was reasonably certain there was an oil derrick slowly pumping up and down, another non–sequitur for the California I assumed I knew.

"Late model Chrysler," Vasily replied. "Over a hundred thousand on the odometer. Did a VIN lookup and found it had nothing interesting in the accident department, though it did have several outstanding recalls from the manufacturer."

"Oh?"

"Yeah. Four: an airbag issue, something with the starter, an update for the cruise control computer." He looked up. "Wanna guess what the fourth one was?"

"Malfunctioning rear seat?"

"Bingo. But since Chrysler had notified the family of the defect – and they did, we have a copy of their mailing records – their liability ended there."

"I'm starting to see why they are going after your department," I nodded.

"Somewhat deep pockets, yes," Vasily agreed as he tapped the edge of his notebook against his jaw. "Though the parents didn't strike me as the litigious type. I think it's more their lawyer, actually."

"He sees a big payday."

"*She* does," Vasily corrected. "Martinez and Lobowitz are the premier firm in this part of the state if you want multi–million–dollar payouts from the boys in blue."

"So, the lawyer approached them?"

"That's my impression," Vasily said carefully. Only the faint trace of color on his cheekbones clued me in.

"Damn, Vas," I swore. "Really?"

Vasily twisted away from me, his face flaming intensely. "I don't know what you're talking about," he said.

I stepped over to him and put a hand to his shoulder, turning him to face me. "Tell me everything, right here, right now," I said softly. "I can't help you with one arm tied behind my back."

Vasily angrily twisted his shoulder out from beneath my touch. "What makes you think I need help?" he said testily. "I've been doing just *fine* without you."

"The view is quite different from where I'm standing, Vas."

"Is it? I didn't know you could see *anything* from that cloud–shrouded pedestal of morality you're on."

I stepped backwards like he'd hit me in the gut. "Hey now," I said, hands half raised defensively. "I'm not judging what you did––"

"Like *Hell* you aren't," he said. "You may not be saying it in so many words, but I know you better than most."

"I could say the same," I replied softly in an attempt to defuse his emotions. Not normally prone to anger, I worried that much like my friend Mike, California had done some damage to my friend. There were likely wounds – and scars – yet to be uncovered. "Regardless of what you might think, you're still my best friend, Vas. Not having spoken to you in months doesn't change how I feel."

I turned and looked up the hill toward the school. "I was reasonably certain that I'd have a chance to run into you as part of the duties of this case." I looked over my shoulder. "While I didn't expect to be bailing you out—"

"I said I don't—"

"—I'm here now, and that's exactly what I intend to do." I turned back toward him. "You *do* know me, Vasily. And you know how I feel about the truth. I'm going to get to it one way or the other, and I'd much prefer to do it with your help."

He glared at me.

I smiled slightly. "I'm not as by–the–book as I used to be these days, so I can roll a bit longer with keeping Mike in the dark about us. But you need to be honest with me right now or I can't help you." I paused, searching his eyes. "I've always trusted you, my friend. Still do. Trust *me* now."

Vasily turned away from me again, forcefully enough that his ponytail snapped around with him. I watched as he crossed his arms against his chest and dropped his chin, then slowly blew out a long breath. Turning back, he had a semi–amused expression on his face. "You really are a sight for sore eyes, you know that, right?"

I laughed slightly. "I'd say the same, but I fear I don't mean it the same way you do."

"True," he sighed. "I'm sorry, Sean. I am in deep. Deeper than I ever thought possible."

"Then we'll get you out. Together."

"Are you hungry?" he asked suddenly. "I know a great taco place, and I can spill my guts to you over a mojito."

I pulled out my iPhone. "We're both on duty," I reminded him as I dialed Suzanne.

"You just said you weren't by-the-book anymore."

"I did," I smiled. "If you can keep it to one, it's on me."

Pressing the phone to my ear, Suzanne's phone rang on the other end. "Sean?" she asked, though the line was crackling pretty badly.

"Hey Suze. I'm not going to make it back for lunch."

"Sean?" she said again. "Is that you?"

Raising my voice, I tried again. "Suze? I'm here. Can you hear me?"

"Sean, look I'm only getting half of your words. If this is you, call back or text." And with that, the line went dead.

Holding my phone out a bit, I could see I had barely one bar of reception. "Lousy coverage down here," I muttered as I texted Suzanne.

"Yes," Vasily said, and the smile in his voice made me look up. "It's next to impossible to make a call from this lot."

I looked at him for a moment. "Is it, now?"

Ten

Suzanne wasn't all that happy that I was leaving her to her own devices and informed me that she was off to Disneyland for the rest of the day, should I care to join her later. Groaning, I texted an appropriately amorphous response before turning my attention back to the conversation at hand. "I'm going to need to see everything on this case," I said thoughtfully. "Especially the cellphone records."

"I figured as much," Vasily said, inclining his head toward the rear of the SUV. "I might have accidentally removed the boxes from the station this morning."

I rolled my eyes. "This is a train wreck, you know that, right?"

"More than you realize," he chuckled as he turned into a strip mall like most I'd been passing since arriving in California.

The parking lot was jammed with cars, which, again, seemed the norm for California; Vasily easily navigated the SUV over the speed humps and managed to score a parking spot a few feet from a nondescript storefront that had a simple sign over the door. "Cafe Cosa?" I read.

"Best spot in town," Vasily said proudly as he turned off the SUV and we got out.

The small place was doing a brisk lunchtime business, forcing us to find a two–top on the side patio that had not been immediately obvious when we'd driven up. As we settled in, a handsome young waiter appeared at Vasily's elbow. "Vas," he said with a slight accent. "How were the waves today?"

"Flat," Vasily said with a smile. "But tomorrow is another day." He turned to me. "Jorge, this is an old friend of mine from out of town; Sean's visiting for a bit."

Jorge turned his dark eyes and matching complexion toward me, a slight question on his face. "*Hola*, Vasily's friend," he laughed. "Are you here long enough to hit the surf?"

I shook my head with a smile. "Probably not, though I don't surf as well as Vasily anyway."

"*Señor* Vasily is a good teacher, no?" Jorge smiled.

"I don't doubt he has that personal touch," I said straight faced.

Vasily smashed my foot under the table, but I could see the confirmation in the slight darkening of Jorge's cheeks. Clearing his throat, Jorge just nodded. "The usual today, *Señor*?" he asked.

"Yes, and the same for Sean, please."

"*Sí*," he nodded and then was gone.

Vasily turned on me. "Seriously?"

"Some things never change," I chuckled.

He sighed. "He's just a friend," Vasily said.

"Who wants a bit more out of the relationship, I think," I replied.

Vasily put his head into his hands. "Can we *not* talk about my sex life right now? Please? Things are bad enough right now without dredging that up, too."

"Fine with me," I said. "So, did you tip off the lawyers?"

Vasily looked up through his hands and a few stray strands of blond that had come loose from his ponytail. "Not right away, no. As the Chief probably told you, through sheer dumb luck I wound up the lead investigator on the case."

"He did mention that, yes."

"I knew immediately it was a shit assignment," he continued. "For my former partner was the lead in the first car that rolled. Interviewing him was a ball of fun, I must say."

"Let me guess, he's the one that thought it was a phantom call?"

"Yes. His partner wanted to do the same sort of grid search I later called for but was overruled and then told to 'forget' he'd made the suggestion."

"Lovely."

Vasily sighed. "I started from the same spot as everyone," he said. "And I was reasonably certain my role was to finish the paperwork and pack everything up as quickly as possible. At least at the beginning, we were all on the same page: it was an accident. A terrible, unbelievably horrific accident, but nothing more."

Jorge arrived and set down two frosted glasses before disappearing again. I picked mine up and savored the rum/lime/spearmint mixture for a moment before smiling. "Not bad," I said as I took another sip. "What was it that made you think to get the lawyers involved?"

He nodded as he sipped his own. "I'm getting to that. Don't rush me."

"Sorry," I said with a smile.

"Little things started to pile up and became big things," he said. "While I'd known about the first car, of course, I didn't know about the disagreement between the two detectives until I interviewed the junior member of the team – Milorad Guernsey. Miles was still hot under the collar and gave me an earful when I interviewed him."

He looked away. "I had to interview Mark, too, and I can't discount the fact that he intentionally distorted his version of the experience due to our prior... connection," he said carefully. "He's made life quite difficult for me. I think he expected me to be fired, not demoted."

"I can't wait to meet this sonofabitch," I said.

"I went to the scene just as we did this morning right after taking their statements and writing my own. Not that there was much to see at that point, but I did our thing and took photos, measured, the works. No 'ah–hah!' clues jumped out at me until I tried to call the parents to set up a time to speak with them."

"No signal?"

"None. I tried from multiple places in that lot, and finally had to walk up the hill to the school before getting enough bars." He smiled wryly. "That seemed odd, given how I'd been told the victim had made multiple calls from his minivan. In that lot."

"Did you verify that?"

"I tried to. I went back to the station and discovered other than the call to Dispatch and the rather nebulous coordinates they'd given both responding vehicles, no one had pulled the cell tower records for the victim's phone."

I leaned on my elbows. "I suspect I'm backing into the answer. But how big an area did Dispatch give you originally?"

Vasily blew out a breath. "About seven blocks, maybe eight. It included the school and part of the mall next to it. And a small medical complex across the street from the school."

"Damn. That's a large area."

"No kidding," Vasily replied. "I don't have to tell you how unreliable the GPS ping is for 9–1–1 when someone calls in on a cell phone. The sheer ground both cars had to cover when they got the call was staggering. What's worse, though, is that the GPS for both department vehicles clearly shows we drove past the minivan."

I thought about that for a moment. "What were you looking for, exactly?" I asked.

"Funny you should ask it quite that way," he replied. "All we got was an 11–30 from Dispatch – incomplete call. Even *they* didn't fully grasp that the kid was dying, though from the tape I heard later, it's hard not to see why in retrospect."

I nodded. "So you wound up driving through multiple blocks looking for something. And if he was pinned below the seat, you'd first have to know he was trapped inside a car and then start searching each and every one."

"I certainly didn't get that when I was called in," Vasily replied. "But I had a gut instinct when nothing stood out that we needed to do a more thorough search. I was overruled, much like Miles was." He looked at me, a pained expression on his face. "What's worse? I don't even remember *seeing* the van. I had to have gone past it at least twice, since I circled the lot."

"You didn't have much to go on. And without something to draw your attention..."

"Exactly. Still, I feel like I missed it."

Jorge returned once more and carefully slid a plateful of colorful food first in front of Vasily, and then me before adding a tray of various hot sauces. "Enjoy," he said with a small bow before disappearing once more.

Hefting one of the well-stocked tacos, I looked to Vasily. "I'm starting to see why you did what you did," I said.

"It mounted up," he nodded. "The more I dug in, the more I saw not only a number of failures on our part, but a real chance that a piece of the story didn't fit with everything else."

"The cell signal?"

"Exactly. I wanted to do a test with the victim's phone to see if it *could* have even made the call. Chief Gilbert was already annoyed with me to start with, though; when I sought permission to test my theory, he accused me of trying to make a crime out of an accident for my own personal redemption."

"He shut you down?"

"Completely. At that point I'd already talked to the family. They are good people, Sean. And their son is dead. It's rocked their universe, and the best the department could do was some trite condolence card and a quick close to the case."

My eyebrows rose. "Hang on. Do you think there's a crime here?"

Vasily nodded slowly. "I do."

"You already told me the car had a recall. So, what, criminal negligence on the part of the parents?" I asked, shaking my head. "That doesn't fit with how you've framed the story."

"Not the parents, no," he said softly. "You still need to talk to them, so I won't paint any details there just yet. I will tell you though, I'm convinced that minivan wasn't in the parking lot when I drove through; I'm also reasonably certain it wasn't there when the first SUV passed, either, though I don't have enough evidence on that yet."

I blinked. "Did I miss something? I thought he was found in the minivan. In that lot."

"He was," Vasily nodded before he took another bite of his taco.

I blinked again. "You think... you think he died somewhere else? Within the seven blocks of the cell tower zones?"

"Yes."

"He couldn't very well have driven himself to that lot," I said, frowning.

"I agree."

I put down my taco. "Are you trying to convince me that for reason or reasons unknown, Chase Cromwell was... killed? And then his body was placed in that parking lot?"

"By one or more people, yes," Vasily nodded.

"Is there any evidence of that?" I asked, a bit stunned. "Trace or otherwise?"

"I have no idea." Vasily sighed as he sat back and laced his fingers behind his head. "The van wasn't searched, fingerprinted or anything. We handed it right back to the family as soon as we thought we were done with the case."

"Did you bring any of this to Chief Gilbert?"

"Yes. I wound up on desk duty."

I leaned back in my chair, the remaining tacos untouched on my plate. "And *then* you called the lawyers."

"Yep." He looked at me. "I wanted to rattle the Chief – *needed* to rattle him enough to take another look at the case. I didn't expect him to call you, though. That was an unanticipated stroke of good luck – the first I've had since landing in this Hell hole."

I stared at him. "That's pretty thin stuff, Vas."

He smiled at me. "But it's got you thinking, hasn't it?"

"That's not the point! This is messed up! And it's most definitely *not* how you get an investigation started!" I said defensively, but I knew my face had betrayed me. For what he had described did, at the very least, bear some further scrutiny. I couldn't deny my curiosity had been piqued.

Vasily smiled wider. "Damn. I *have* missed that."

"Missed *what*?" I asked with some exasperation.

"Watching those gears as they start to move," he said with a wicked gleam to his eye.

I sighed and put my head into my hands. "Fine. But if we do this, we do this my way."

"I would expect nothing less," Vasily said. "Oh, and one more thing."

I glared at him. "What?"

"I managed to get the minivan shrink wrapped. The family wants to know where to send it for analysis."

Eleven

I agreed to meet up with Vasily first thing the following morning at the same coffee shop, then took the files from him and headed back to Anaheim for the afternoon. Far too much had happened too quickly for my tastes, so the first order of business was to review the materials on the case up to that point. While I plowed through that part, Vasily planned on getting the paperwork ready to pull the minivan in for a more thorough going over by the crime techs. I had little hope that anything might still be left to discover, but then again, you never really knew what to expect with the lab geeks got a chance to do their thing.

The drive back to the hotel went much smoother in the early afternoon – so much so that I risked calling Mike on my Airpods. He picked up on the first ring. "Sean? I thought you'd pop in at the station at some point today."

"Sorry, Mike," I laughed. "You know me. I jumped right in with both feet."

"Ah," he replied cautiously. "Any breaking developments?" he asked with a nervous laugh.

"Not really. I'm going to take a run at the case files this afternoon and tonight. Then I'll start walking through the witnesses."

"Witnesses?" Mike replied. "Like the officers?"

"Exactly," I said, noting how he had reacted to my intentional use of the word. "I might talk to the parents tomorrow, too. Just to get a sense of the family."

"That's probably not necessary," he said quickly.

"Still," I chuckled. "It feels like the right thing to do."

"They're suing our asses, Sean," he said rather hotly. "I think you can skip the social visit."

I waited a beat. "Mike, are you actually directing your independent investigator to avoid a subject of interest?"

He paused. "No," he said carefully. "Of course not. Do what you think is best."

Mike's tone indicated he didn't exactly feel that way, but I chose to push on. "I'll want to circle back and talk to you tomorrow if you are free," I said instead. "You can buy me that drink you promised then."

"Sounds good," he replied quickly before hanging up.

I found our room deserted after schlepping the boxes up to it on a borrowed luggage cart. As I ran the cart back to the Bell Desk, I called Suzanne who picked up on the first ring. "Please tell me you've not eloped with Bugs Bunny," I said.

"It would be *Mickey Mouse* for this park," she laughed. "And so far, I've managed to dodge his advances. But I have to say, Aladdin is getting a second look."

My eyes widened as I stepped over to a quieter section of the lobby. "Suze, if memory serves, he's a teenager..."

"Not the twenty–something playing him this afternoon," she laughed harder. "Don't worry, I've not fallen head over heels for him quite yet. So long as you still meet me for drinks and dinner at Downtown Disney."

"I can do that," I said. "I've got an hour or more of files to peruse; what time do you want to meet?"

"I already have reservations for two at a pizza place I found. I'll text you the location – meet me there at 5:45?"

"5:45?" I chuckled. "That's pretty specific."

"What can I say? It's Disney and their militaristic precision."

"'Theme park' and 'militaristic' don't exactly go together."

"You'll understand once you've experienced it properly," she replied. "Don't be late."

"I'll be there, love," I replied.

She blew me a virtual kiss over the open line before clicking off. In an attempt to ensure I stayed in her good graces, I set a reminder for our dinner on my iPhone as I headed back to the hotel room to dig into what Vasily had provided me.

The Anaheim Marriott appeared to have been built over the course of a few projects, expanding beyond the original main building to several connected towers and its own rather giant convention center. One thing Anaheim didn't appear to lack was convention space, especially given as the Hilton across the street made a similar offering; it's sleek, modern glass–and–steel structure seemed more thematically unified than the apparent build–as–you–go mentality of the Marriott. Our room was on the second–to–the–top floor of the optimistically named Oasis Tower, with windows looking directly at megalithic Anaheim Convention Center itself. As I entered our room and tossed the keycard down on the counter by the television, I stepped to the window and pulled back the curtain to take in the visual once more.

I'd been told at check–in that the road directly in front of the hotel and the convention center adjacent had only recently become a pedestrian parkway. In true Southern California fashion, there were planters everywhere overflowing with colorful flowers; a circular fountain with jets of water resided almost in front of the massive set of doors that represented the main entrance to the conference space. Palm trees, gaily decorated with lights that came on at dusk rimmed the space, and I knew from our stroll the prior evening that space–appropriate music was piped in over speakers hidden among the foliage. While not technically part of the Disney experience, the entire area had an exotic resort feel that had a tendency to make one relax – even if it was just a few miles from the interstate.

Letting the curtain fall back, I moved to the small desk in front of the window and opened the first box. There was a scattering of files inside, along with a thumb drive that had the logo for the Rancho Linda Police Department. Deciding to go digital first, I grabbed the drive and slid the box to the side so I could pop open my MacBook.

It took me a few minutes to dig through my backpack in order to come up with the correct dongle allowing me to connect the drive to my laptop. I often wondered if my penchant for Apple devices was some sort of penance for misdeeds I had accrued in a past life, for I had spent a fortune in adapters after this latest hardware upgrade. Still, it never stopped me from upgrading to the next shiny version when possible.

Vasily had scribbled the passcode to the files on a sticky note, and soon I had multiple virtual folders open across the desktop of my computer. The first contained a tranche of photos from what I now thought of as the crime scene; some I had reviewed when Mike had called, but others were there from angles that were new, including one shot that included the entire profile of the minivan. Immediately I understood why Vasily was so certain he'd not missed the van his first time through.

Clearly the van had experienced a rough life, for there was a sizable dent running the entire length of the passenger side; it had exposed the white undercoat of the vehicle, a long gash that stood out against the darker navy blue of the siding. Memorable for sure – and it would have easily been visible as anyone turned into the lot, given where it had been parked. I found myself shaking my head, though, for even as much as it *had* stood out, there would still have been no reason to have been looking specifically for it. At least, based on what I knew; Vasily had been specific in that the callout had been for "citizen in distress," a catchall code that assumed the issue at hand would be readily apparent to the responding officers. The van – visibly empty – wouldn't rise to that level.

I clicked through the rest of the photos of the minivan, which the crime scene photographer had carefully ensured covered every possible angle and any detail that seemed unique. From the missing wiper blade on the dusty rear window to the uniquely shaped parking sticker for the high school, nothing had escaped their attention. I closed out the viewer and dragged the folder to the side; below it was a set of audio files, which I assumed were the communications from that day including the original 9–1–1 calls. Part of me didn't want to review those, but the professional side won out and I queued up the first call in iTunes.

"*9–1–1. What is the nature of your emergency?*"

There was some sort of response, but it was so faint, I couldn't hear it. Apparently, that was also the case for the operator.

"*9–1–1. What is the nature of your emergency?*"

Again, there wasn't anything audible. The operator tried a third time.

"*9–1–1. Please state the nature of your emergency.*"

There was a pause, and then I heard her address something to (presumably) a supervisor.

"*Cell phone call, Sergeant. I can't get a response, but it's an open line. Should I roll?*"

The conversation didn't get picked up by her microphone until she came back.

"*If you can hear me, we are sending officers to your location.*"

She waited maybe ten seconds, and then the call ended.

I rolled the cursor back and replayed the call, turning the volume up as high as the laptop could go. I presumed the same had been done by the initial investigating officers, so it wouldn't hurt to hear whatever they had heard. Still, even cranked to the max, it was hard to determine if anything was at the other end of the line. I rolled it back multiple times, and at best I *might* have heard something like a whisper in a few places, but it was so faint as to be confused with just normal background noise.

Hitting pause on the recording, I stared at the waveform on my screen. Even if Chase had been capable of pressing the seat far enough off his diaphragm to breathe, I was starting to wonder if he'd been too far away to use the voice–activated digital assistant in the way the original investigators had thought. I sat back in my chair, for that led to another insight. Digging through the paperwork, I located the inventory from the van and noted the phone was indeed in the cupholder on the driver's side. Tapping the hotel pen to my chin, I realized it couldn't have been on speaker mode – that required a manual action on the phone – so even if Chase had managed to summon Siri, he well may not have heard – or known – his call had gone through.

Closing out that audio file, I pulled open the next one. It was similar to the first call to 9–1–1, and also ended with the operator again rolling a vehicle to check. If the background noise *was* Chase, he was barely audible in the first few minutes of the second call; by the end, it was impossible to hear anything from him, forcing me to assume he had finally succumbed at that point.

Poking through the assets folder on the laptop, I found the transcripts from both and nodded, for it confirmed even the experts at the crime lab had been unable to glean any useful conversation from the recordings. If anything, seeing the emptiness of Chase's final moments in black and white made the entire situation all the more appalling.

I set aside those audio files and saw there were more – presumably the callouts from Dispatch to the two cars that were sent to the scene. I set those aside for a moment and dug further for the cellphone records. It took a second for me to locate the original report generated by the 9–1–1 operator, and a little more time to pull up the proprietary software we used to plot geographic coordinates; unsurprisingly, the seven–block circle that Vasily had mentioned appeared in a light orange on the map overlay.

Tapping my pen to my chin again, I scanned the map. It wasn't terribly difficult to see where the cellphone towers that had pinged the phone at that moment might have been, nor was it hard to determine the sheer amount of ground the two vehicles were forced to cover when they'd been dispatched to the scene. Vasily was right – there was a massive mall on the northeastern part of the zone, the school and its grounds were on the southwestern part, and the strip of buildings with a sizable parking lot smack in the middle had to be the medical complex.

Scanning back through the paperwork, I tried to find any sort of clue that they knew *what* they were looking for. Nothing about the call to 9–1–1 had indicated that Chase was trapped, let alone trapped within a vehicle. For all they knew, the officers were looking for someone passed out on the sidewalk. From that perspective, the department certainly had a reasonable excuse for why they'd not been able to turn up anything, though admittedly their searches had lasted (I checked the clock times on the reports) nineteen minutes for the first vehicle and thirty–seven for Vasily.

Sorting back through the virtual files again, I sought out the records of the cellphone itself. For many of my investigations, requesting records around a particular time of interest was routine, but I quickly found that the flash drive had nothing. Returning to the physical world, I dug through the paper files and came up empty. Unboxing the second storage container didn't reveal my sought–after treasure, either, so I punched up Vasily on my personal phone.

"Chief," he answered on the first ring.

"I just noticed you never changed your Maine number," I said with a smile. "Is that a sign you missed me?"

There was dead silence for a moment, and I realized I had inadvertently stepped on a live wire. Hastily I covered my mistake. "Listen, I can't seem to find the cellphone records for Chase. Do you have them at the station?"

Sounding relieved, Vasily answered. "No, actually. The case was closed before we had to pull the data. Why?"

"Just a hunch," I said thoughtfully. "Can you get them?"

"It depends," he said, and he lowered his voice. "We'd need a warrant, but that would require re–opening the case. Have you found anything that would merit such an action?"

I turned back to my computer and clicked around until I came up with the long shot of the minivan. "Maybe," I replied. "I don't suppose you asked the parents how the van came into possession of that dent?"

"It's more of a long gouge," Vasily corrected, "though the shadow from the angle of the sun makes it look worse in our photo. But no, I didn't. Remember, this was pretty much shut down nearly as soon as it started. We didn't get a chance to ask too many questions of anyone."

"Then we talk to the parents first thing tomorrow."

"I've already set the appointment for nine. Coffee at seven?"

I smiled. "I'll see you then."

Hanging up, I found my eyes tracing the long, white line on the side of the van. It felt like a lead for some reason, but I wasn't entirely sure why.

Twelve

Needing to think, I asked the front desk at the hotel how far a walk it was to Downtown Disney. They quickly handed me a Marriott–branded map and directed me toward a lovely garden pathway that ran between the Convention Center and the Hilton across the street. Compared to Maine, the low sixties at that part of the evening felt warm as I set off to meet Suzanne.

Walking beneath the now–lit palm trees, I thought I could see the direction Vasily had been hinting he wanted to go in. For it was clear to me now that there were more than a few gaps in what little of an investigation had been conducted. I still needed to review the transcripts of the calls between the detectives and dispatch, not to mention their interviews conducted later, but at the core the entire case felt skewed to the side somehow. And the very fact that I was thinking of it as a case, and not just a consulting gig looking into professional conduct, told me something as well.

I needed the cellphone records and the embedded location data, that much I knew for sure. As I crossed Katella Boulevard and ignored the screams of joy from the rollercoaster that ran along the sidewalk behind some tall bushes, I intrinsically felt that Vasily was right. Chase had died someplace else and had been moved to the location where he was found. The *why* was still beyond me, but that wasn't unreasonable given the lack of information I had at my fingertips. Perhaps more troubling, though, was *someone* had taken the time to drive the vehicle – with a dead or dying Chase inside.

At the very least, that made it a possible case of manslaughter. And that would blow the hinges off the quiet little investigation Mike Gilbert had called me in to do. Maybe having drinks with him in the evening the following day wasn't such a great idea after all. Not until I had a much better idea of what I was getting into.

Fortunately, I'd left my service sidearm in the safe at the hotel, but did forget to take my badge off my belt before passing through the metal detectors at Disneyland, triggering a secondary screening by a grandfatherly–looking supervisor with a wide–brimmed hat. I could easily tell he was an ex–cop by how he held himself, not to mention the general aura each of us seemed to exude to the public. Making the ob-servation to him brought a deep rumble of laughter, and led to a brief swapping of horror stories as he manually waved his small wand over me, followed, oddly, by an offer of a job at retirement.

"I'm a little young to be thinking about that," I laughed as I re–clipped my badge to the belt.

"As soon as you get your twenty in," the officer smiled. "Call Casting and tell them Bob sent you."

"All right," I chuckled as I waded into the crowd, one eye on my iPhone and another looking for signs leading to the restaurant Suzanne had chosen.

Right at the stroke of 5:45 I found the love of my life standing at an outdoor host podium. She smiled as I leaned in to kiss her. "Inside or out?" she asked.

"Outside, if they have heaters."

"Done," she said and looped an arm in mine.

As we entered through a double–glass door beneath a clownish fig-ure holding a pizza paddle, I turned and arched an eyebrow. "Naples?"

"As in Italy," she explained as we crossed through a small dining room and then exited the far side of the space onto a sizable patio crammed with tables full of people. The smells of oregano and fine cheese intermingled with fresh dough. "The house specialty is hand tossed thin crust pizza, baked in a wood–fired oven. Or you can have pasta. I figured I could cover both bases pretty easily, depending on how your day went."

"If they have sangria, I may never leave."

"The best in the park," the hostess replied with a smile. "It's our own recipe."

"Well done," I laughed.

The waitress appeared immediately after the departure of our hostess, carrying a small basket of fresh bread and a canister of olive oil. In mere moments, we'd placed our drink orders and were perusing the pizza menu. "I'll eat almost anything save for anchovies," I reminded Suzanne. "So, get whatever you want. But save room! I think I saw an ice cream parlor on my walk through."

"I saw it too," she said. "And the candy shop across the way."

I groaned. "This is a disaster zone for anyone wanting to eat sensibly."

"People are on vacation when they are here," she pointed out. "Who diets when they travel?"

"You sound like my mother," I laughed. "That would have been her take on it, I think."

"Sounds like a solid woman in my book," she smiled and turned as our waitress re–appeared with our drinks. "This size," she said, pointing to something on the menu. "The three–meat version – with extra cheese?"

"Of course. Anything to go with it? An appetizer?"

"The ricotta balls, please."

"Excellent choice. Those will be out shortly."

I looked out over Suzanne's shoulder and the bustling crowd moving to and fro. Despite how crowded the area was, it didn't feel overwhelming; the gentle curves of the walkway seemed to keep the volume flowing, more or less. Trees and colorful plantings were everywhere, and a vibrant underscore of music surrounded the space from unseen speakers. "This is far different than when I was here last," I said as I sipped my sangria. The hostess was right – it was insanely good.

"To be fair, you spent most of it inside the hotel, right?"

"Yes, save for runs to get food."

"Well, this is the third or fourth iteration of Downtown Disney since it opened. The newer of the two parks has gone through a sizable makeover, too. And they just added a massive new land themed to *Star Wars*."

I choked on my sangria. "*Star Wars*? Since when is that Disney?"

Suzanne laughed. "Quite some time. Disney bought it from George Lucas and made a number of new films. How did you miss all of that? They were huge hits – well, most of them."

"You have to ask me that?" I rolled my eyes. "The person you had to introduce to *Miraculous Ladybug*?"

"I need to work on your pop culture a bit more, I think. Next, you'll tell me you have no idea who Harry Potter is."

It felt best to stay silent.

"Dear Lord," she sighed as she sipped her wine. "Speaking of *Miraculous*, I'm planning on wearing my outfit to the keynote tomorrow night. Are you still game?"

"I am," I smiled. "I'll need some help getting into costume."

"I think I am up to the task. How did it go today?"

I sipped at my sangria, giving myself a few moments to formulate an answer; fortuitously, the waitress chose that moment to appear with our appetizer. After divvying up the small set of deep–fried cheese balls, I smiled slightly. "Speaking of *Miraculous*..."

Suzanne raised an eyebrow. "I believe that was my line, stranger," she laughed.

"Yeah." I paused for a moment, wondering why I was hesitating. "I ran into Vasily today," I said simply. "Actually, it's more than that. He's been assigned as my partner for this case I'm working."

Suzanne's fork paused in mid–flight, her eyes wide. "You told me he'd moved back to California," she started. "You neglected to mention he worked in Rancho Linda."

I put my fork down. "I did."

She popped the mouthful of cheese and pastry into her mouth and quickly swallowed. "You know, most *normal* people would have been rather excited at the chance to catch up with an old friend. A best friend. They might have even mentioned it to their girlfriend, too, so she could, I don't know," she paused, waving her fork in the air, "maybe put together a dinner outing. Or something."

Suzanne wasn't wrong. And just like that, she'd managed to get right out into the open what had been nagging at me for days now. I'd assumed there would have been a chance of running into Vasily – actually, if I were being truly honest with myself, I'd *hoped* it would have been more than a chance. For I rather desperately missed my friend.

As someone whose career depended on truth and honesty, I'd been strangely capable of lying to myself on that one point. More troubling was my inability to understand why.

"It's... complicated," I said weakly. "Yes, I knew he worked out of Rancho Linda, but I assumed I'd be able to carve out time to connect with him while working on the case."

"Hang on," she said, eyes widening. "You didn't tell him you were coming?"

"I didn't have to," I shrugged. "It wasn't a secret who Mike was bringing in."

Suzanne stared at me. "And he didn't call you, either?"

"No," I said.

She put her fork down. "You told me you were best friends. *Are* best friends."

"Yes."

"I must be missing something. For it sounds to me as though today was the first time you two have talked since he left." She paused, seeing the look on my face. "You've got to be kidding."

"No," I replied, feeling at turns defensive and appalled at myself. "It's complicated," I said again, "but it was also at his request."

She snatched her wineglass by the stem and took a long drink, her jerky actions telegraphing her increasing anger. Putting the glass down, she blinked and then fixed me with a soft expression. "I never asked exactly what went down between you two that day at Maine Medical.

Why Vasily suddenly disappeared after being by your side for a decade and a half. But the nuttiness surrounding the idea you'd fly me across the United States and then wait *another* full day to tell me he was here makes me think it's time for me to hear the story. Finally."

I smiled wryly. "The whole story?"

She smiled grimly. "Every last gory detail. Warts and all."

I sighed, and took a large drink from my sangria in an effort to brace myself. "It's pretty simple, I suppose, although I'm not sure how he would feel about me telling all of his secrets to the competition."

"What competition?"

I inclined my head toward Suzanne. "You."

Suzanne sat back, her ire suddenly dissipated. "I... I don't understand...?"

Toying with my glass, I sighed again. "He's in love with me. Has been for years." I looked up. "I was completely unaware of how he truly felt until late last year; when I did find out, though, I managed to crush his heart pretty soundly."

Suzanne blinked. "He's... gay?"

I shrugged. "As long as I've known him, yeah. It's partly why he wound up living in Maine; his family disowned him as a teenager for his 'abhorrent lifestyle choice.' I met him on the swim team at UEM."

"Wow," she breathed. "It's the new millennium for crying out loud! Were his parents luddites or what?"

"Definitely. I've never met them, thankfully. Otherwise, I'd be likely to explain to them just how out of step with society they are."

"No kidding." She reached for her glass again and took another healthy sip.

"Anyway, during the Pelletier case, we had a moment in a hotel room in Boston –– stop smirking, Suze – and it became crystal clear to me that all of his innuendo was actually heartfelt."

She nodded slightly. "That must have been the heart crushing you alluded to."

"Yeah," I said, hanging my head slightly. "I love him, of course, but not the same way he apparently feels about me." I looked up. "I think of him like a brother – as family, really. And my tastes have never run in the same direction as his, if you will."

"I see," she smiled a bit more. "Good to know."

I let her comment pass. "He made the call that staying in Windeport would be untenable once he realized there was no chance he could change my mind. So, he left."

"And asked you not to call him?"

"Pretty much."

She reached a hand across the table and held mine. "I had no idea, Sean. As I said, I knew he was special to you; having him up and vanish overnight had to hurt." She paused, and then added, softly, "But you could have told me sooner. There was no reason for you to suffer in silence."

I put my other hand over hers. "It was an open wound that I thought had finally healed," I said quietly. "Until today." I looked at her, hard. "You know I love you. Deeply and passionately. Right?"

She smiled again. "I do," she said softly. "But I realize it's possible to have love in your heart for someone else, too. Maybe not of the same *order*, but just as deep. And," she added carefully, "how it can be just as passionate."

I felt my eyes watering, and I blinked it away. "I'm not sure until this afternoon I realized how much I missed him. And how terrible I've felt about hurting him." I looked away. "I really didn't know, or what's worse," I said even more softly as I turned back to her. "I *did* know and chose to ignore it. For fifteen years."

Suzanne looked down at the table, a wry smile to her face. "I'm not perhaps the best person to dole out advice, for I was pretty blind when it came to my own love life. Sometimes you only see what you want to see." She looked up. "There are times," she said, tapping her finger against the back of my hand, "times when we can't see something, even when it's right in front of us. We're blinded because it's simply outside our frame of understanding."

I nodded.

"Put another way, you're built differently than Vasily. Wired up from another plan. As you even said, you *did* recognize his overtures toward you – the 'innuendo' you called it; but from your perspective that's all it was."

I felt my face warm. "And I like to think I'm an enlightened man," I sighed again. "But even I fell prey to social preconceptions, didn't I?"

"Not entirely," she said. "The very existence of your friendship speaks volumes of your ability to accept and affirm others that are different from yourself." She reached a hand up to my face. "And not all of this is on you, love. Vasily had to have known fairly early on you were unattainable. Yet he persisted."

In a striking bit of introspection, I nodded again. "Much as my pursuit of Deidre."

"Exactly," she smiled again. "Often we keep going after our dreams and desires long after we know we'll never reach them."

"That sounds crazy," I said.

"That sounds like being *human*," Suzanne laughed.

"So, what do I do, Doctor?" I asked honestly. "I can't deny that being drawn out here to California was some sort of karmic opportunity to settle matters."

"Maybe it is," she answered. "Though it feels like it might be more complicated, given he's partnered with you for a bit."

"True. And he does seem different. Living out here has changed him, and not necessarily for the better."

Suzanne leaned in and kissed me quickly. "Then maybe your arrival was meant to remind him of the person he once was – and of who the two of you were to each other, once. And could be again, if either of you boneheaded jocks could see past your internal hurt."

I laughed. "There it is," I said appreciatively. "The unvarnished truth."

"Not quite," she smiled as she drained her wine glass and signaled the waitress for a refill. "For that, I'll require a few more of these."

Thirteen

Somewhat unironically, Vasily was in the same exact booth I'd shared with Mike the previous day. He was in a polo shirt emblazoned with the Rancho Linda Police Department logo, the tight–fitting technical fabric accentuating the fact that he clearly had continued to work out. His hair was damp and in a partial flip ponytail, and as I slid into the seat opposite, I caught a whiff of the cologne he had worn for years.

Except he'd not been wearing it yesterday.

It was a sign, and one that put me on guard. The last thing I wanted was to misread the situation, or worse, for me to inadvertently make an overture I'd not intended to be seen as such. Being more cognizant now of my effect on him wasn't making it any easier, though; I caught him smiling warmly at my appearance before suddenly remembering where we stood with each other and shifting his gaze back to the menu he'd been holding and masking his expression once more. In that brief, unguarded moment, though, I'd seen enough to realize I'd need to tread very carefully.

I had no desire to hurt him again.

He looked at me over the top of the menu. "I can't believe you want to eat here," he said as his eyes went back to the menu. "Everything is deep fried, or doused in pure sugar. Even the eggs look questionable."

"Hey, I'm not from around here," I said as I held my hands up defensively. "Besides, *you* were the one who said we should meet here, if memory serves."

Vasily started to protest when a striking waiter approached; he had an odd haircut, with one side of his head shaved, and the other sheathed in shoulder–length dark hair. "Dude," he said with a smile that exposed his piercings. "The usual?"

I shifted my gaze to Vasily, who smiled faintly. "Yeah, thanks Drew."

The waiter nodded and turned his eyes on me, and I noted he was wearing strange contact lenses that masked the pupils. "What can I get you?" he asked pleasantly as he scribbled Vasily's order down on his pad.

"Western omelet and a coffee, black, please," I replied after a quick scan of the morning options. Vasily wasn't kidding, hardly anything on it could be done without a grill or a vat of hot oil. At least the coffee appeared safe.

"Wheat or white for your toast?"

"Wheat," I said, trying to convince myself it would offset whatever horror my omelet was about to be cooked in.

"Got it," he smiled. "Back in a jiff with the coffee."

I turned back to Vasily, who shrugged at my unasked question. "He's part of the Master's swim team I'm on here," he explained.

I felt a half smile appear. "Uh–huh."

"Honest!" Vasily said defensively. "He's one of only a handful of people I consider a friend of sorts out here. They were hard to come by, that's for sure."

"So it seems," I replied. "Look, Vas..."

"Oh, here it comes," he sighed, rolling his eyes as he leaned back and placed his arm across the rear of his seat. It was hard not to stare at his bulging bicep. "Chief Colbeth trying to make peace with something he's uncomfortable with."

I found myself caught a bit off guard by his sudden shift in temperament. "You never used to be this dramatic."

"I've been through a lot, Sean. Especially since leaving Windeport."

"I know, but—"

"Can we not do this? Right this moment?" he asked. "Whatever is wrong between us can wait until we've gotten to the bottom of this case."

I shook my head. "I disagree. I think where we stand with each other is a *huge* factor in how successful this investigation will be."

"Then we will have to agree to disagree on that point. There is nothing to talk about."

"I'm not sure that's true."

"Let's just stick to the case? For now?" It held a note of pleading.

I looked at the man who had been my friend for so many years and saw the turmoil in his eyes. There was plenty to discuss, and no little amount of pain hiding behind that pleasantly impassive expression he was training on me. Slowly, I nodded. "All right. But only if you promise we can dig through this before I go back to Maine."

He nodded, though I wondered if it was more to shut me up than anything else.

Still skeptical, I let it drop. "Clearly you already have a theory of this case," I started. "And that you feel strongly it's not just a case of death by misadventure."

Vasily nodded slightly. "I do."

I waited for a long moment, and when it became apparent he wasn't going to add anything, I crossed my arms and glared slightly. "You could save me a lot of time by simply bringing me up to speed."

That made him look out the window. "I... have to admit to some level of concern that I'm seeing something where nothing exists," he said to the glass and the cars whisking by on the street outside. Turning back to me, I could see he was wearing a bit of a concerned expression. "I guess I wanted an independent confirmation I was on to something." He waited for a beat, then very, very quietly asked: "Am I?"

"How can you doubt yourself?" I asked in return. "You're a top-notch investigator."

He rolled his eyes. "Not according to my Chief," he laughed ruefully.

I looked at him again, and saw none of the self–confidence he'd once carried with him as a second skin; instead, he exuded the nervousness of a fresh–from–the–academy patrol officer. I decided the case could wait for another moment. "What the hell happened out here?" I asked, concerned lacing every word.

"Plenty," he said softly. "But it's not relevant." He looked at me for another long second. "Am I on to something?"

I smiled slightly. "Yes," I nodded slowly. "From what I've reviewed so far, I'd want a few more questions asked. And a few more rocks lifted in order to peer beneath them. To get a clearer picture of the circumstances surrounding the death of young Chase."

Vasily blew out a breath. "I still think we screwed up initially," he said. "But I also don't feel like either of the responding cars had a fair chance."

The waiter appeared and put down a steaming mug of coffee and a thermos jug beside it. I couldn't be sure, but I thought he winked at Vasily as he moved away to the next table. I hid my smile just in case.

Stirring in some sugar, I continued. "I tend to agree on that point, but we need more data. The cell records will help us confirm a bit more specifically where the calls were placed but based on our own experience, I'd have to think it wasn't from that lot at the school. And if *that* is true, it means he was moved."

"Why to the school? In order for the body to be found?"

"Maybe," I replied. "It's likely where he was supposed to be at that hour anyway, right?"

Vasily nodded. "Based on what the parents said, yes."

"And when did the father find him?"

"Four hours and change after the first 9–1–1 call."

I tapped the spoon inside the mug. "So that means we have about a four–hour window," I remarked thoughtfully. "Perhaps... perhaps the minivan was moved precisely because he'd *not* been found."

Vasily blinked. "Holy *shit*," he breathed. "I'd not thought of that."

"It does change the frame bit." I sipped my coffee and smiled slightly again. "I'm willing to wager that whoever made the call to 9–1–1 assumed that, like the movies, police officers would roll to the exact location in no time flat." Placing my spoon down on the napkin, I asked: "And are we sure that Chase made the call?"

A wry smile played at Vasily's lips. "We didn't have a reason to run a test. The phone was in the front seat and had made the calls; it was a given he'd been on the other end."

I smirked. "You live in California, land of smoke and mirrors."

He shook his head. "You Maine people are so cynical."

"Yes," I agreed. "But it makes us great cops," I continued as our food arrived. "Eat up so we can get out of here. I want to take a spin through the cell zone before we meet the parents."

Vasily did a mock salute. "Of course, *mon capitaine*," he laughed.

It was the first normal thing I'd seen him do since my arrival in California.

Fourteen

Why I was surprised that the Cromwells lived in a McMansion on the outskirts of Rancho Linda was beyond me; I chalked it up to my detective reflexes being fuzzy due to the time change. For some reason, though, I had assumed a kid who had scored a full–ride athletic scholarship would come from a family housed in one of the weary sub-divisions I'd been passing in my travels through the area. Instead, they were living on a hill that provided sweeping views of Rancho Linda be-low, settled into a nicely sized lot terraced against the elevation. It was peacefully bucolic, save for the oil derricks further up the road.

Vasily parked his SUV on the angle at the edge of the rounded drive-way and the two of us walked the semicircular pavement to the double door beneath the dramatically hung lamp. I paused outside the white doors and took a moment to appreciate the effort that had gone into making the house appear to be decades older than it really was.

Hollywood was everywhere in this state.

Ringing the doorbell brought on the cacophony of dogs barking, followed by a masculine voice hollering. I smiled a bit more as some things were the same no matter whose door you knocked on. A moment later, a somewhat older version of Chase greeted me. "Chief Colbeth?" he asked as he extended one hand while using the other to hold back a large chocolate lab. "I'm Parker. Parker Cromwell. Please ignore Huston – he thinks everyone is breaking and entering."

"A pleasure, Mister Cromwell," I said as I shook his hand. "I believe you already know Detective Korsokovach. I'm sorry to meet you under these circumstances." I leaned down and scratched Huston behind his floppy ears. "And you too, Huston."

"You've just made a friend for life, Chief. And call me Parker, please."

"If you'll call me Sean."

"It's a deal," he smiled. "This way, gentlemen."

We followed him past a massive twin staircase straight out of *Sunset Boulevard* and down a short hallway to a small study; a cherry desk sat in front of a big bookcase with two guest chairs facing it. To my surprise, a big, bulky IBM Selectric typewriter in powder blue had pride of place on the desktop, a page partially rolled up. On the opposite end was a cozy tableau of a couch and two recliners, all angled toward a gas fireplace. "This is my favorite room in the whole place," Parker confessed as he took the couch and waved us to the easy chairs. "I'm a writer by trade, and I do my best thinking right here."

"Screenplays?" I asked.

Parker laughed. "I wish. No, I'm a science journalist, right now with the *Times*."

"Oh! My apologies," I said, a bit chagrined. "I have to say, this house gave me the wrong impression."

He laughed. "This——" he waved his hands at the house around us, "is a result of a book I published a few years ago about a rare virus in South America."

I blinked. "You're *that* Parker Cromwell?" I said suddenly.

"You know my work?" Parker smiled.

"I happen to be dating a doctor who does," I replied. "I have to admit, it was a gripping read. Especially the way you forecast how the southern part of Mexico might become a hotspot."

"Accurately, I'm afraid," he replied sadly. "Look, I know we have an active lawsuit pending against the department. But as I'm sure the detective has told you, despite what our lawyer wants, my wife and I were only hoping to get the Rancho Linda Police Department to take another look at what happened to my son."

"You don't think it was an accident?"

"I don't know *what* to think, other than it wasn't investigated for shit," he said and then smiled thinly. "Sorry," he apologized. "Chase was our youngest, and my only son. It's something of an open wound that won't heal."

"I can understand." I glanced knowingly at Vasily, who shifted slightly to retrieve his notebook. "Are you comfortable talking with me? After all, *technically* I represent the best interests of Rancho Linda. Not you or your family."

Parker looked to Vasily. "If what the detective has told me about you is accurate, and Google would seem to indicate that, I feel like I am in good hands. So yes, I am comfortable talking with you. What questions can I answer?"

"Right off the top, would you be willing to release the minivan back to us? I'd like to run some further forensics on it." I paused. "It would go faster if you agreed, but we can also go—"

"Absolutely," he said. "I've kept it isolated in the garage – none of us have been in it since it was returned to us by the department."

"Vasily mentioned that," I smiled. "We'll have a tow truck pick it up today, then."

"Good."

"Now, about that gouge on the door – do you know when it happened?"

"Had to be sometime on Saturday," Parker replied.

Vasily coughed. "I'm sorry?"

"All I'm saying is it didn't leave here with it. I assumed something happened to it when the department transported it." He paused. "It's part of our lawsuit."

"Interesting," I said as I looked to Vasily. "And Chase often did the optional Saturday workouts?"

"He did." Parker smiled warmly at a memory. "Chase was an excellent player, Sean. I have no skills in that department, though my wife was a gymnast at UCLA. He had to have picked up all of that talent from her. Our eldest daughter got the writing gene from me."

"What's the age difference between your kids?"

"Six years," he said quickly.

"So, she's not here, then?"

"Oh no, she works for a textbook publisher in Oakland and lives there with her husband. He's a computer guy for a firm in the Valley."

I glanced to Vasily. "As in Silicon," he added.

"Ah." I tried not to look chagrined.

I took in our host once more and in the slightly different light of the study, could see I hadn't been all that off in my initial impression. While Parker had the thin lines of middle age around the eyes and corners of the mouth, his face and deep blond hair were a near match for the teenager I'd seen in the photos. The round glasses and more conservative haircut did little to hide the resemblance he had to his son.

"Forgive me for asking this," I said as I made a point of gesturing at the space we were sitting in. "Your house speaks to the success you've had as a writer and journalist. And yet your son was to be a recipient of a full–ride scholarship, correct?"

Parker smiled ruefully. "That he was. You're not wrong – I *have* been successful, but not enough to provide my children with the financial backing to attend anything more than one of the lesser–known state schools." That caused him to frown slightly. "I've a mind to have my colleague on the investigative finance team take a look at the true costs for higher education. My daughter received a partial academic scholarship herself; we funded as much as we could, comfortably, but she left with a hefty amount of debt."

"Ouch."

"Indeed," he nodded. "We thought about selling the house and downsizing, and had even brought someone in to give us an accurate market valuation. It came in lower than we expected, but what equity we had might have allowed us to send Chase to UCLA. Then the scholarship came through."

"When did he get tapped?" Vasily asked.

"Last fall." He smiled fondly at the memory. "His high school had one of those 'letter of intent' ceremonies, since Chase is – or rather, was

– the first tennis player recruited in more than twenty years. It was a big deal for the community, at least for a few days."

"None of his teammates were actively recruited?"

"Not really," Parker said. "One or two are close to Chase's level, but there are so few slots the competition is pretty tight."

I glanced at Vasily and he nodded slightly. "Chase was well liked? He had friends?"

"Quite a few," Parker replied. "I'd have to look at his phone to give you their names, but to be honest he moved in a few different circles. He was a top scholar *and* a high performing athlete. That tended to bring together an unlikely group of kids cutting through the scholars and the jocks."

"That's unusual," I agreed. "Would you mind, actually, if we borrowed his phone? We'd like to review it a bit more as well."

"Sure," he said cautiously. "You won't remove anything on it, will you?"

"Absolutely not," Vasily replied. "We have the ability to clone everything on it, safely, and then can return the original device to you."

"Good," Parker said, a bit relieved. "I know this probably sounds awful, but I've been replaying his voicemail greeting a few times each day. It's the only recording I have of him, if you can believe it."

"In this age of social media and smartphones?" I asked, eyebrows raised. "I am a bit surprised."

Parker smiled wryly. "I'm a writer, not a videographer. My wife has thousands of photos, but not me. Just memories."

"Did your son have any social media accounts?" Vasily asked. "He might have left behind some additional audio or video."

Parker looked a bit shocked. "He does, yes. I never thought about that, actually." Something flashed across his face. "I don't know if we can get into it, though. I have no idea what his password was or any of that. My wife might, though." He inclined his head toward the classic IBM Selectric typewriter on his desk. "I'm probably more old school than most parents."

I chuckled. "I've only ever had a word processor," I admitted. "The first time I had to actually type something was when I filled out a requisition at the Department. It didn't go well."

"It's an acquired talent," Parker laughed. "I like the physicality of the act. I can truly *feel* my writing as I create it – a sort of direct connection to my work I can't get when I use a computer."

"I think I can understand that," I smiled as I glanced at Vasily. "One last thing before we chat with your wife – would you allow us to pull your cell records for the day of the... uh, rather, the day your son died?"

Parker frowned. "I thought you had those already?" he asked, looking to Vasily. "You did request them the first time."

I turned and saw the shock on Vasily's face, which he covered quickly. "Do you remember which officer had you sign the release?"

"Yes," he said. "Because it wasn't an officer. It was Chief Gilbert himself."

Fifteen

Vasily and I took a quick moment in the garden just outside the study before interviewing Adele Cromwell. Sliding the glass door shut, I lowered my voice to ensure it wouldn't carry. "I gather from your expression just now that was an unexpected tidbit of information."

"It was," he said equally as quietly. "I'd assumed he was going to say Mark had asked for it, hoping maybe for some ammunition I could use against that S.O.B."

I frowned. "Mark would be your former lover?"

Vasily flushed a bit. "Mark Freidman, yes. He was the lead in the first vehicle, and contacted the parents while I was working the scene. It was his case until Chief Gilbert abruptly handed it to me."

"That is a bit of a non–sequitur, then," I said as I shook my head slowly. "Based on what Mike told me his own assessment of your skills were, giving you the case would have ensured it would get a thorough going over. Yet he suddenly closes it? And *then* calls in an outside investigator to see what the department might have done wrong?"

I walked the edge of the small patio and leaned against the brick half–wall. "This makes no sense. It's almost as if he's been torn between *truly* examining the facts and trying to save face for the department. Which is it?"

"My money?" Vasily said as he crossed his arms. "Aside from how he's treated me personally, from what little I've seen since he joined the department he's generally been fair and incisive. How he's handled this case is a bit of an outlier."

I nodded. "I've known him for years and his reputation is exactly that." I looked out and up the hill to the house that loomed large on the terrace above the Cromwell McMansion, and realized the owners would be able to see just about anything going on below them. I couldn't see myself living in a situation like that. "Until we know more, we have to assume Mike asked for and then for some reason buried the cell records. Since we've asked again, let's get them again; maybe we'll discover why he's not brought them to our attention."

"Got it. Just as soon as we're done here."

"Good," I said as I looked back through the glass doors. A strikingly beautiful woman had appeared and was sitting on the couch next to Parker. "Let's get back to it, then."

Adele greeted our entrance with the nervous smile most people wore when they faced a cop. I had long since gotten used to how people reacted once they knew what I did for a living, though in some cases, studying their reactions also tended to give us more information than they generally intended. Where Parker had been completely at ease with us, Adele was fidgeting slightly, twisting the hem of her shirt between her folded hands. "Mrs. Cromwell?" I asked pleasantly as she started to stand. "Sit, sit, please," I smiled. "I'm sorry to interrupt your day with more questions."

"It's not a problem, truly," she said. "Did Parker offer you anything? Coffee?"

Her husband looked a bit chagrined. "I did forget my manners, Allie," he said before turning to us. "Can we get you anything?"

I smiled a bit wider. "We're fine," I said. "And I don't want to keep you. But it's quite kind of you to offer."

"Are you sure?" Adele asked, more perhaps so she could escape the room for a few minutes. "It's no problem at all."

"Coffee, then," I replied.

"Same," Vasily added.

"Give me just a moment," Adele replied as she bolted from the room as quickly as a well-bred hostess could manage.

Parker looked after her and then turned back. "She's been a bit uneven since Chase died," he apologized. "She's a nurse, actually, but has been on leave since the... incident. I don't know if she'll ever go back at this point."

"That is not unusual in these sorts of circumstances," I said. "Why do you think it's affecting her?"

"Chase was very close to his mother," Parker said. "Much closer to Adele than he was to me. Don't get me wrong, I loved him deeply and we talked all the time. But the truly sensitive conversations were always with his mother first."

"That, too, isn't unusual," I said. "At least, my friends tell me kids sometimes have a stronger connection with one parent than another."

"You don't have children, Chief?" Parker asked.

"No," I said. "I have some nieces that I spoil – well, used to spoil," I said sadly. "But no kids."

Parker was poised to ask more when Adele bustled back into the study with a small tray. Four mugs were arrayed perfectly around a small creamer and jug of sugar. "Here we are," she said happily.

I grabbed a mug and handed it to Vasily, then picked a second one up. The coffee was weak and watery, confirming my suspicion she'd fumbled the settings on a second-rate Keurig. I could see from Parker's expression that I was on the money in my assessment, but nonetheless smiled at Adele. "Wonderful, thank you," I said.

"My pleasure," she said, and the smile started to give way again.

"I was asking your husband earlier about Chase's friends, and he mentioned you might have access to your son's social media accounts. Is that the case?"

Adele shot a look of panic at Parker. "Yes," she said haltingly. "I have access to his password vault – it was our deal when we allowed him internet access at age thirteen."

"Part of what I want to do is fill out a better picture of your son, Mrs. Cromwell," I explained. "Reviewing his posts, who he had as friends, the sorts of subjects he followed – those will help me to understand who he was, and how he related to the world around him."

"I don't quite understand how that would help you look into the accident," she said.

"Frankly, I'm not sure yet either. Often I don't see a connection right away. But I'd like the chance to look if you'll allow me."

Adele looked to her husband again. "If it will help…" she said.

"It could, honey," Parker said.

"All right," she nodded. "I'll get the password vault key. Will you want his laptop, too?"

"If you wouldn't mind. Vasily will give you a receipt for everything that we borrow so you can keep track of what you've loaned us."

"Okay," she agreed, though it was tentative at best.

We chatted for another quarter of an hour, but it was clear we'd gotten as much out of her as we were going to at that point. A few minutes more and we had the cellphone, laptop and passwords for everything and were on our way out the front door when Parker stopped me. "Sean," he said, ensuring we were out of earshot of his wife, "I'm not a cop, but from what Detective Korsokovach has already told us – and what he's purposefully *not* – it feels like there is more to this than just an accident. Is that… is that the angle you are looking at? Or are you truly only reviewing the way the Rancho Linda department handled the situation?"

Trying to skirt the line a bit, I answered carefully. "The two aren't mutually exclusive, Parker. While my goal – and the reason I am here – is to look into how the officers handled your son's death, I'm also following any new leads that develop as a result."

His eyes popped open. "Have you found any… leads?"

"I can't really say," I replied. "But I assure you I'll be in touch as much as I possibly can."

"I'd like that very much," he said. "Vasily speaks very highly of you, by the way. Enough that I feel like we're in good hands here."

I smiled slightly. It had been some months since anyone had thought that back in Windeport; hearing it from a relative stranger sparked a reaction I didn't realize I'd missed: being valued. "He flatters me," I replied sincerely. "Though he is a very capable investigator in his own right. I wouldn't be here if he hadn't started to dig around the edges, to be perfectly honest."

Parker nodded. "Then maybe, between the two of you, we might get some sort of resolution to this gnawing hole Adele and I are dealing with."

"We'll do our best," I said. "And we'll be in touch."

Sixteen

Still somewhat jet lagged, I hadn't realized how long we'd been at the Cromwells until Vasily asked if I wanted to catch lunch before heading back to the station. A quick glance at my phone told me we were at half past eleven. "I would," I said, "but I'd like to get a run in first. I didn't work out this morning and could really use a few miles to clear the brain."

"Not swimming anymore?" he asked.

"I do, but not with the team," I admitted. "It became uncomfortable after the Pelletier case."

"Really?" he asked, surprise in his voice. "Why?"

"As it turns out, you might have been the smarter of the two of us," I laughed ruefully. "For it seems our small village is not overly fond of having its secrets exposed, even if it's in the pursuit of justice."

"Did you bring your workout gear with you?" he asked, his voice tight.

"Yeah, it's in the rental."

"Then we run. I know a nice park not far from the station. And you can tell me *exactly* what went down after I left."

The station wasn't much further, and we rode the rest of the way in tense silence. For some reason, I could sense that Vasily was upset, but at what I wasn't entirely sure. As he careened around the turn into the back lot at the station and swerved into an empty spot on two wheels, I wondered which one of us would be served better with a short run.

Vasily took the laptop into the station with the intent of having the techs print it and clone the system; it was a standard process used nationally, so I assumed the machine would be available for me to peruse later that afternoon. I wasn't entirely certain if the prints would come up with anything interesting, given how much time had elapsed since Chase's death, but you never knew. At that point, it felt prudent to do everything by the book.

I detoured to the rental and grabbed my duffle bag out of the back, then followed Vasily's retreating form through the rear entrance of the station. And there I waited until my partner returned to take me to the sizable locker room with showers and storage compartments just off the rear entrance. Vasily snapped open a spare locker and then crossed to one that was his; it wasn't lost on me that the handful of officers that were in the space made a point of abruptly stopping their conversation and quickly evacuating from the room while pointedly ignoring Vasily. One had hastily thrown on his polo and khakis without fully toweling off from the shower and was trying desperately to jam his foot into a loafer as he rounded the corner of the exit.

I couldn't help but call out at his receding form: "Really? What is this, nineteen–eighty?"

A single raised middle finger was the only response.

Turning to my friend, I waved at the now–empty space with steam coming out of my ears. "How long has *that* been going on?"

"Some time now," he said, and I could see it had beat him down a bit. "Despite living in California, this particular part of the state seems to be a little less forward thinking than most. It got worse after I broke up with Mark."

"I want names," I said, only half kidding. "I'll remind them what—"

"Sean," he said with a half–smile. "As much as I appreciate the fact that you still feel that way, I don't think it would help matters."

"It would make *me* feel better."

"For a bit," he laughed. "Come on. Change so we can get out of here and have lunch."

I hurriedly stripped out of my informal uniform and donned some running tights and a comfortable tank–top; needing a pocket for my phone, I added complementing microfiber shorts. Snapping a lock on the door, I turned; Vasily had tied his hair back with a spandex–like head covering favored by pro football players and was just tugging on one of those compression tank–tops, something even with my own reasonably well–defined physique I was unwilling to wear. "Ready?" he asked as he laced up his sneakers.

"Yes," I said as I noted his footwear had the same tri–color combination as his running tights. Color coordinated as always. "How far do you want to go?"

"I usually do a ten–k myself at lunch," he said, a slight bit of competitiveness entering his smile.

"You're on," I replied as I donned my sunglasses and followed him back out of the station.

There was a well–groomed pebbled path at the rear of the parking lot that fed into a shady corridor of trees; I started the workout on my watch and fell into an easy pace next to Vasily. "How bad is it?" he asked.

"It seems a bit unfair of me to spill my own tale of woe without some sort of reciprocal agreement in place," I jested, "but it's bad. I'm a pariah in the very town I grew up in."

"For real?"

"Yeah," I said, turning slightly to see the streaks of sun wash across his face. "I wasn't kidding. The general consensus wasn't 'great job, you solved the case.' It was more of the 'what possessed you to lay bare the town unto itself.'"

"You were doing your job," he reminded me. "That has to count for something."

"That appears to be the thin line that originally kept me employed, but a few weeks back I got caught in a shoot-out while trying to serve an Eminent Domain notice."

"You... *what?*"

I smiled wryly. "It sounds worse than—no, actually, it *was* bad. Bethesda Thompkins wound up taking her own life in front of me before I could stop her, and that seems to have been the final straw for the Village Council." I glanced at him before returning my attention to the trail. "I've had a hard time replacing your position, and it led to me being out there without backup. It's being viewed as a serious lapse in judgement. That's on top of our dear friend Yvette Bedard suing us over her conviction."

"Shit. *Shit.*"

"Yeah. The forces arrayed against me don't quite have the votes on the Village Council to remove me as Chief, but I was told shortly before flying out here that might not last much longer."

"You don't sound very optimistic."

"I'm not," I sighed (as best as I could, as Vasily had surreptitiously stepped up the pace). "I've not told Suzanne exactly how thin the ice is I'm on, though she has seen enough on her own to know the mood of the village with respect to me."

"After all the years you've been there? I can't believe they turned on you like that."

"That's what happens when the lawyers take over," I said wryly.

"Can I assume, then, you've not buried the hatchet with Charlie?" he asked as we rounded a gentle downward curve and started up a slight rise.

"You can," I said. "That's on me, too. I've bumped into her at the grocery store a few times, and though we're civil, it hasn't gone beyond that yet." I looked at the small pond we had started to circumnavigate. "I miss seeing her kids. I miss her cooking."

"You did press her pretty hard during the investigation."

"That I did. I make no apologies for how I handled the case, Vas."

"Maybe you need to," he observed as we crossed a viaduct. Ducks were serenely swimming along a canal that appeared to feed the pond; for some reason, I thought it was odd that they had ducks in California.

"For what?" I asked. "The questions had to be asked."

"Not by you, though," he reminded me. "You could have had me be the heavy."

"That's never been my style," I replied.

"I know," he laughed slightly. "One of many things I love about you."

We came to a wider part of the path and I pulled up. "Love? Or *love*?" I asked as I stretched a bit. "This feels like an important distinction we need to make."

Vasily paced around me in a circle. "I didn't want to get into this with you," he said softly, hands on hips.

I smiled just a bit. "You know me," I replied as I watched him pace. "Once I get ahold of something, I pull the thread all the way."

Vasily was breathing hard, the muscles in his chest rippling beneath his compression shirt with each intake – as if I'd needed any further evidence that we'd been pushing hard. Finally, he stopped pacing and stood a few feet in front of me. Wiping his face with the back of his hand, he finally looked up. "Yeah," he said simply, "you do."

"Moving away didn't help, did it?"

Hands back on hips, he glared at me. "No," he said tightly. "Are you happy now? Is that what you wanted to hear?"

"It's not," I said gently. "And I am most *definitely* not happy."

"I'm sorry," he said, blowing a breath out. "Just about everything has gone wrong since I arrived in California." He looked up at me and pushed back a stray lock of hair that had escaped his head scarf. "I really thought a clean break and a change of scene would help me get over you. That putting physical distance between us would equate to emotional closure."

He inclined his head toward the trail and I fell into step beside him once more; this time, the pace was not world–record quality as we slowly jogged our way through his emotions. "I was so desperate to replace the hole in my heart for you, I eagerly jumped into something with Mark despite the sensible part of my brain screaming it was a bad idea."

"Because he was a co–worker?"

"Not just that," he replied as we started up another short rise. "I think on some level I was using it as a rebound, and it blinded me to Mark's actual motives for hooking up with me." He laughed a bit sarcastically. "He realized immediately I was a danger to his career; my credentials had been impeccable upon arrival, and put me slightly ahead of him in the promotion line. He waited to make his move, though; he was a plotter, that one." He looked at me sideways. "The day after Mike arrived to replace the Chief that hired me, Mark landed in his office and accused *me* of inappropriate sexual advances on the job – that I had forced him to sleep with me and then tried to keep it quiet."

I raised my eyebrows. "Mike must have seen through that," I replied. "He's a damn fine detective."

"It didn't matter," Vasily fumed. "Department policies are pretty clear; a reprimand and demotion were pretty much mandatory, and I'm on notice that one more screw–up will result in termination."

"That seems harsh," I said. "Especially for someone with such an impeccable record."

"I suspect that's all that saved me from being let go then and there," he replied. "As I said, Mike is pretty fair; he saw the work I'd done up to the... incident... and took that into consideration." Vasily smiled slightly. "I won't lie, the demotion stung; but there was a bright spot. Mark's plan backfired; instead of getting me out of the way and clearing his career path, he also got demoted and reassigned to a new partner."

He started to jog again, and I followed him. "So, to answer your question, yes, at the end of the day, I still know I love you. And that love has quite nearly ruined my career."

Stunned into a bit of silence, I tried to absorb what he'd said and process it. Indirectly my actions – or inaction, rather – had triggered the series of events that landed me on that running trail next to my best friend. I could no longer deny our relationship was extraordinarily more complicated than I'd realized. I also knew I needed to figure out a better way to fix it – or redefine it in a way that both of us could live with.

Intuitively I knew it would be one of the hardest cases I'd ever tackle.

"Your departure hurt me more than I thought it would," I said suddenly.

Vasily skidded to a stop on the pebbled pavement and looked at me, hard. "That wasn't my intent—" he started, a crease of worry on his face.

"I know it wasn't," I replied. "Whatever I felt was definitely not your fault in any way, you must understand that. And to be honest, I'm not sure I actually realized what had happened to me until very recently."

This time I started jogging and he was the one to fall into step. "For weeks afterward, I found myself coming up with reasons to call you and then would talk myself out of them. The few times I did call, you never answered, so it became easier not to try. So, I buried myself in the work as I am wont to do, but that was another problem entirely for it had been years since I'd had to fly solo."

I smiled a bit. "As if I'd needed any confirmation, I think Suzanne was the one who pointed out we were two halves of the same brain. With you gone, I was on my own. And it felt *wrong*."

"You must have replaced me."

"I tried," I sighed. "But after two rounds of failed interviews, I gave up. There were good candidates in there, but they weren't *you*." I looked at him as we started down a long hill. "And I wanted *you*, plain and simple," I grinned slightly, "though not, perhaps, the way you want me."

"It's nice to be wanted," he said softly.

"That part has never been an issue for me," I replied. "You're my best friend, Vas. I've always wanted you in my life."

"Part of me knows that," he said. "It's just not enough."

"I know. I knew after that night in Boston, but even as enlightened as I am, I didn't have any idea how to address it then; nor do I now." I looked at him with a sad smile. "I'm sorry for what you've gone through out here, Vasily. It's not an excuse for my own actions, but I at least wanted you to know there was pain and agony on this side of the equation, too."

I paused at the bottom of the hill. "I'm open to any ideas as to how we move forward. Together. For this is not working for either of us right now, I can tell you that for sure."

"It's not," he replied, hands on hips. "Damn, Sean," he said. "You really can draw stuff out of people, can't you?"

"I can," I smiled as I held out a hand. "I don't honestly know what we can do, but I'm here for you now and I'm gonna make this work. Somehow."

He took my hand and that sly gleam I used to see in his eyes appeared for a moment. "It would help if you had a twin brother that I could hook up with," he laughed.

"I don't, sadly," I said as I pulled him into a brief hug. "Let me save your ass and then we'll figure out the rest. How does that sound?"

"Like the best plan I've heard in weeks."

"Good. Now, how far away is lunch? Because I'm starving."

Seventeen

Only in California did it seem completely ordinary that the two of us would enjoy fast-food burgers and fries clad in spandex still damp with sweat. And yet, that was exactly what we did at a joint called In-n-Out Burger that was perched at the end of the running trail. I'd questioned the sensibility of having greasy food and then needing to run the three miles back to the station, but Vasily assured me we'd go slower.

Knowing he was lying, I opted for carbohydrate loading and ordered two of the cheeseburgers on the amazingly simple menu, then stood back as Vasily requested some strange combination of toppings that were not to be found anywhere on the placard. As we settled in over the small tray of wonder that arrived at our table, I looked at him questioningly. "How on earth did you know they would put grilled onions on if you asked?"

"They have an entire secret menu here," he smiled. "You'd be surprised exactly what they will do, if you know what to ask for. I found this location a week or so after moving out; they are all over the place, much like McDonalds is back east. Best burgers in town."

Unwrapping the wax paper embracing my first cheeseburger, I took a bite and was pleasantly surprised. I'd watched them make French fries from solid potatoes while I was ordering, and sampling a few of those raised my eyebrows as well. "Not bad," I said.

"Another few days," he said with a smirk, "and I'll have made you a true Californian."

"Not likely," I laughed as I snarfed down the first burger. "So, the case," I said as I dabbed a fry in a pile of ketchup Vasily had made in his own tray.

"Hey!" he said loudly as he shifted his tray out of reach.

I ignored the glances that came in our direction and smiled. "Force of habit," I said.

"You never stole from me in the past," he said, arching an eyebrow.

"It's a new day," I laughed. "I've got to meet with Mike when we get back. I'm thinking of bracing him about the cell records. You want to be there?"

"Absolutely. I should have called impound to retrieve the minivan before we left, though. Let me make that call before we see him?"

"Sounds like a plan. I'm going to go through his social media this afternoon and maybe after dinner—–*shiiiiiit!*"

Vasily raised his eyebrows again. "Forget something?"

"Yeah," I shook my dirty blond curls barely restrained by my sunglasses. "The comic convention I'm going to with Suzanne starts tonight. I promised her I would go. But I'd started down the path of asking if you wanted to assist with the social media... what...?" I asked as I saw a sly expression on his face.

"I'm going to that myself," he said. "Do you need help getting into costume? I can grab my gear and follow you back to Anaheim."

"Suzanne was going—"

"I love your girlfriend, but she did a terrible job of getting that mask on the last time out."

"How do you know I'm using—"

"*Of course* you are," he said as if it was the end of the discussion. "We'll have to leave here no later than three to miss the traffic, though."

"Okay," I said unsure what I had just agreed to. "Now that we have *that* settled, did you do any digging into his friends? More of his background? I feel like I have a picture of how his parents felt about him – his father, especially." I played with a fry for a moment. "His mother, though... she was concerned about us accessing Chase's social media, wasn't she?"

"I didn't do much background on Chase," Vasily answered as he quickly polished off his second Frankenstein of a burger. "It's an area that needs some development. I'll set up an appointment tomorrow at the school. Maybe by then, you'll have spelunked through enough of his online life and we'll know what kids to look for." He took a sip of his diet soda. "As for the mother, yeah, she was acting strange enough that I *really* want to know what's in his online persona."

"Then I'll race you back to the station," I grinned as we stood and tossed our trash into a bin on our way out of the small burger place.

Despite lunch sitting like a rock in my stomach, we made excellent time on the returning five kilometer run to the station; to my surprise, Mike Gilbert was waiting for us at the rear door to the station. "Sean," he said before turning his cool gaze on Vasily. "Detective, I need you to run to the courthouse and pick up a warrant for the Devereaux case."

Vasily kept his face impassive, but I could see him curl a hand into a fist. "Let me change—" he started.

"*Now*, Detective," he said.

If he was trying to prove something to Vasily, I was at a loss to understand what it was. "Mike, at least let him shower. I can't believe you'd send him to a judge's chambers in workout gear." I paused, laughing slightly. "I certainly wouldn't."

Mike turned his steely gaze upon me. "The judge is waiting, Detective. I need a word with your former Chief."

Vasily started to object and I waved him off. "We'll regroup when you return," I said casually.

"All right," he said tightly before turning on heel and jogging across the lot to his SUV.

Mike pulled me off to the side and away from where a small crowd of his officers had paused to see his confrontation with Vasily. "I'd appreciate it if in the future you didn't challenge my authority in front of a junior officer," he said.

"Shit, Mike," I said a bit loudly. "You intentionally sent a multi–year veteran on a milk run. You wanna explain to me why you think a sweaty, spandex–clad detective is the best image this department can project to a judge?"

"I remind you you're a consultant working for *me*," he said icily. "You're not here to judge the way I run my own department."

"Good to know," I replied. "So, why did you send him?"

"I have my reasons," he said as he turned to go back to the station.

"I'll be meeting with you in an hour," I said to his receding back. "I have some questions."

He paused, hand on the door to the entrance. "I'm sure you do," he said without turning, then disappeared into the station.

Eighteen

A little after one, I was cooling my sneakers in a small conference room adjacent to Mike's office. My MacBook was open on the table and I'd begun going through the social media accounts while I waited for Vasily to return. I had this sixth sense that the situation was going to get more complicated at the station and knew having a second witness with me at all times would be beneficial; for that reason, I'd delayed meeting with the Chief and had instead camped out in the conference room directly after my little chat with Mike, still clad in my running gear to imply solidarity with Vasily.

Vas had texted me that the judge in question had been held up in court, so he was similarly in a holding pattern at the county courthouse a few blocks away. A quick check of the judge's busy docket upon his arrival had been illuminating, and had proven his assignment had been some sort of odd penance for misdeeds as yet not understood. In short, there was no way for him to know exactly when he would be able to return to the station.

The password vault Adele had provided access to was a cloud–based system; logging into it, I could see Chase had been very active online, with accounts configured all over the known internet universe. Pulling on gloves, I'd slid his laptop out of the protective bag we'd placed it into and powered it on; I tried to ignore the fingerprint dust that seemed to have gotten into every key and under the keyboard.

Like most teenagers, there was no password on what appeared to be a fairly current MacBook Air. It booted directly to the main desktop, which had a shot of what I could only assume was some sort of video game. I didn't play myself, but Charlie's kids had a gaming console and had exposed me to the genre. Idly, I recalled that Vasily had been a huge gamer at UEM, using it as a way to decompress from the stress of being an All–American Student Athlete bound for the Olympics. I smiled a bit, thinking perhaps I could use a bit of that in my life even now.

A quick scan of Chase's installed applications didn't turn up anything overtly nefarious, though there were a few that I didn't recognize. I marked them down in my notes and then started to look through his files. Fortunately, most of his material was local to the computer; it had been my experience that many ordinary users tended to not make use of cloud storage options, save for folks who inadvertently turned on that feature. Cloud vendors often insisted that investigators obtain a warrant to retrieve data stored there, so that was one less complication to be dealt with. Hundreds of folders were present, organized quite effectively into categories that were easy to follow.

Scanning through the academic folder revealed he had participated in many group projects and had written a number of papers over his time in high school. I pulled one up in his word processor and read through it a bit; I was surprised to see his language skills were remarkably good for a student of his age and chalked it up to having a writer in his family. I randomly selected another paper and found it was similarly beautifully written.

Setting those aside, I pushed through folders that had spreadsheets for science assignments, and presentations that he had presumably given. All were crisp and efficient, and totally in line with a student that I'd been told was academically gifted.

The photos folder was empty save for the desktop photo, which seemed odd; as an Apple user myself, I knew that the iCloud system made a constant synchronization between the user's phone, cloud and desktop systems. Chase's phone was still in a small plastic bag, and I unlocked it with the PIN Adele had provided; my eyebrows went up further when I saw it, too, had no photos residing in storage at all.

I may not have had kids, but I was socially aware enough to know that snapping candid photos was second nature with teens and their smartphones. I also knew that the photos could only be cleanly deleted if done from the phone; if I was lucky, whoever had erased them might have missed that key aspect of the iOS operating system.

Scrolling the applications on Chase's computer, I took a chance and launched his browser, then logged into his iCloud account. A few moments later, I was looking at the Recently Deleted folder and the nearly fifty gigabytes of photos there. Scrolling quickly through them, I couldn't be sure, but they seemed to have been wiped on the day Chase died. Fortunately for us, iCloud kept deleted items for thirty days.

Taking snapshots of the date of deletion with my own phone, I quickly highlighted everything and started the long process of restoring them. Within a few moments, they began to appear inside the photos folder on the laptop, though I knew it would take hours for the entire set to download. I made another note that we'd need to find out who had deleted them – and what was within those gigabytes of memories someone didn't want us to discover.

There was one last folder that I poked into, and to my surprise, it looked like an exact clone of the documents folder I'd looked through already. That nearly made me quit digging, but just to be thorough, I randomly opened a file and started to scan it. Reading through it felt like I'd caught the same file already, so I closed it and tried another. It, too, felt familiar; this time, I kept it open and clicked into a third. My eyes widened as I realized I was reading nearly the same content, though subtly shifted in tone and structure.

If I'd not spent the last hour reading Chase's work, I might not have recognized his touch. And yet, clearly these three papers were his though they were designed to *not* seem like his style. I tapped my phone against my chin. This was an anomaly. And I detested anomalies.

My iPhone buzzed and I slid the icon sideways to answer. "Please tell me you're on the way back?"

"I am," Vasily said, chuckling. "Turns out, Judge Spencer is a fan of spandex. He may or may not have invited me to drinks anytime I want."

I rolled my eyes. "That didn't work out quite as well as Mike would have wanted," I said, trying to keep my voice down.

"Likely not. Find anything while I was catching up on my celebrity gossip?"

"I have," I replied. "But I'll tell you more when I see you."

"All right," he said. "Let me run through the shower and I'll join you for our meet–and–greet with the Chief."

"Skip the shower," I laughed.

There was a pregnant pause. "Please, *please* tell me I've not just missed out on an hour of—"

"I'm in the conference room. Come straight here, please," I laughed.

"There in less than five," he said.

Nineteen

Mike stared at the two of us across the faux wood of the conference room table, his face coloring a deep purple. "Are you actually *accusing* me of something, Sean?" he asked, voice icy.

"No," I said as I rearranged my sunglasses against my curls. "I'm just wondering where the records are, Mike. I'm sure it's just a simple case of them being misplaced."

"Can't Detective Korsokovach locate them for you?" he asked, his eyes once more drifting down to Vasily's very visible six–pack under the muscle top he was still wearing.

"I did check through all of the assets for this case," Vasily said evenly. "There is no entry in the evidence log noting the arrival of the records. Is it possible you never received them?" he asked carefully.

I tried not to blink, for there was *exactly* that entry in the logs, and wondered if Vas was trying to catch him in a lie of some sort.

Mike looked at us for a moment, made a decision, and pushed up from the table to move through the connecting door to his office. A moment later he came back with a manilla envelope. "I just remembered," he said flatly. "It was mixed in with my normal mail, and I never got it down to you."

"Ah," I said, ignoring the fact the envelope had clearly been opened. That gnawing in my stomach that Vasily might have been right about my mentor grew by an order of magnitude. "See? A simple misunderstanding."

"Exactly," he replied. "Now, do you want to bring me up to speed?"

"Yes. But first, can you tell me again why Vasily was demoted?"

Vas started and swung his head in my direction, but at my look remained silent.

Mike glared. "I don't see the relevance to the case you're working."

"It could," I replied evenly, "for it seems to have led to a series of mistakes in this case."

"What are you talking about?"

I flipped through some pages on my laptop. "According to your own personnel records, Detective Korsokovach here is your top investigator. And has been since his arrival last fall."

"I never said he wasn't a good detective," Mike replied defensively. "He's just made a few poor judgement calls that have me questioning his ability to be in a leadership role. And he broke department policy."

"Mm–hmm," I murmured. "Which policies were those, again?"

"I fail to see where you are going with this, Sean," Mike said tartly. "And it's highly inappropriate for us to be discussing any of this while he's in the room."

"Gotcha," I nodded. "So, it wasn't because of his relationship with Mark Freidman, then?"

Mike stood up and deliberately moved to the conference room door and gently closed it, then returned to his seat. "This doesn't leave the room."

"Of course not."

Looking to Vasily, he nodded slowly. "Mark Freidman filed a sexual harassment complaint against Vasily the day I took over from Chief Andrews," he started. "I won't go into the details other than to say it was a complicated time for the department – something Detective Korsokovach would attest to."

"It was," he replied.

"From my perspective, the complaint felt vindictive, but the Department has rules that I am bound to follow. Much like yours does, I'm sure."

I nodded.

"Combined with Vasily's open admission to Chief Andrews that he'd had a relationship with Detective Freidman, the complaint had undue weight. There were enough mitigating circumstances that allowed me to sidestep termination, thankfully," he smiled slightly, "and more than enough wiggle room to let Detective Freidman know I thought his complaint was bullshit."

"Hence his demotion."

"Exactly." Mike looked at Vasily again. "Your record is what kept you here, Detective. But you should know that Detective Freidman is making noises that you are attempting to blackmail him with some sort of compromising video. If he lodges a second complaint against you, I'm not sure I'll have any choice but termination."

"That sonofa*bitch*," Vasily pounded the table with his fist. "He's using that against—"

"I don't think I want to know anything else," Mike said softly. "If I had to guess, though, he's mainly pissed off about the demotion and blames you." He looked seriously at Vas. "He's like a wounded animal that's cornered, Detective. Tread carefully."

"Thank you for being candid, Mike," I said, shooting a meaningful look at Vasily. I could see from his expression he was only barely mollified; I could tell that building back trust between him and his Chief would be an uphill battle. Knowing Mike as well as I did, though, allowed me to read between the lines; it was clear he knew Vasily was a valuable member of his department, and would do what he could to protect him.

To a point.

"Again, I would appreciate some discretion on this topic," Mike replied.

"Of course," I continued. "Now that we have *that* cleared up, I have some movement on the case. The minivan is on its way to the lab for a thorough going over, and I've started to review Chase's laptop."

Mike looked at me, hard. "I wanted you to look into the department's handling of the case, Sean," he started. "Not the case itself."

"You can't separate the two," I replied. "I think how the department handled the case is a result of the very elements that I believe make this a bona fide case."

Mike slowly leaned back in his chair. "*Shit.* What did we miss?"

"A lot," I said. "I'm piecing it together now, but I will need a bit more of your resources to do it."

He crossed his arms and frowned. "Tell me what you have," he said.

I took a few minutes to sketch in what little we'd uncovered to that point, some of the key points of the interview we'd conducted with the parents, and then the revelation regarding the gouge on the door of the van. "I'm pretty sure those cellphone records you didn't have will show us the calls from Chase took place geographically *away* from where he was found."

He nodded. "Why do you think that?" he asked. "I'm not challenging your conclusion, but we were reasonably sure the calls had come from Chase. Where we found him," he added looking at Vasily. "Right?"

"It was our working assumption, until I tried to make a call from that lot," Vasily said. "The coverage is bad in that one area of the lot."

"He couldn't have called from there," I added. "But he *did* call from somewhere within the GPS ping we got from 9–1–1. The cell records should tell us what tower he was closest to at the time."

"That would help pinpoint where he was," Mike said, sitting back. "Damn. We all thought it was just a horrific accident." He looked back at me. "Are you saying this was something else?"

I nodded toward Vasily. "Not me. Detective Korsokovach is the first one who figured out Chase was likely quite dead by the time he appeared in that parking lot."

Mike turned to him. "Why didn't you bring this to me?" he asked.

"Would you have believed me?" Vasily replied. "From your perspective, I had one foot on a banana peel."

A shadow of a smile passed across Mike's face. "That is probably true," he said softly as he turned back to me. "And how long have you known Vasily, Sean?" he asked.

"Since college, Mike," I said, adding without hesitation, "and he's had my back ever since. I think, my friend, you might want to take another look at the allegations from his former partner."

Mike laced his fingers behind his head. "Shit. I screwed up, didn't I?"

"Not my place," I said with a smile. "As you correctly pointed out to me today."

He turned back to Vasily. "I knew the whole thing was bullshit," he said earnestly. "But I can't undo what was appropriate under department policy. I'm sorry, Vasily."

"I get it," Vas said with an ironic chuckle. "And I have only me to blame for putting myself into a situation he could take advantage of. Mark's kinda sneaky that way."

"I'm beginning to see that." Mike turned back to me. "Whatever you need, Sean, you've got it."

"Good," I smiled. "Because I think this is going to be rather complicated once we truly start to dig in."

Twenty

"I don't live far from here, actually," Vasily said as we walked to the Convention Center. "Rental housing in Rancho Linda is outrageously priced due to the quality of the school district; despite Anaheim being home of the Happiest Place on Earth, their schools are, shall we say, somewhat less desirable." He laughed, though his voice was muffled a bit by the full-headed mask he was wearing in his guise as Spider-Man. "I still pay close to two grand a month for a one-bedroom apartment."

"That's outrageous!" Suzanne cried. "Please tell me it's more than twelve-hundred square feet?"

"Nope," he laughed again. "About eight hundred. But the location is pretty good; I can see the fireworks from the Disneyland every night from my balcony – if the wind is just right."

"Not a selling point for me," I said. This was the third time now I'd worn my Chat Noir costume, and the first time I'd not tripped over the damn tail right out of the gate. The dark concrete below my boots still radiated with the heat of the day, keeping the chill rolling in from the ocean a few miles west of our location temporarily at bay. The slight nip in the air, though, warned of the coming threat likely to descend upon us later that evening; it was what passed for winter in Southern California.

Vasily had worked his magic once more and managed to get my eyes blackened and mask applied faster than the first two outings; the wig, though, was still hot and itchy, and the way the feline ears were angled made me feel compelled to tilt my head downward slightly as I walked in order to be a bit more streamlined. Still, seeing the excitement on the masked face of Suzanne, enthusiastically wearing her Ladybug costume, was enough to make it all worthwhile.

"I'm glad we're doing this," I said as I leaned into her. "Sorry it had to be as a result of a case, though."

"If that's what it takes to get us to a convention, it's all good," she laughed. "I've never brought anyone with me before, let alone two handsome devils. I'm going to be the envy of all of the cosplayers."

"Then we should escort you properly, Milady," I said with the bow and kiss I'd seen my character do on the show.

Suzanne giggled as I took one arm and Vasily the other; we strolled as a threesome up the courtyard and into the main reception area outside the massive main ballroom. Our badges got us through the next set of doors, and then we parted ways with Vasily for the time being. Having bought his pass months earlier, his seat was many dozen rows ahead of us; ours weren't lousy, exactly, but they were also pretty much in the back third of the hall. What little I could see of the stage made the podium and tables look like dollhouse-sized toys, so as we settled into our seats, I turned my attention to the nearest projection screen instead.

"We'll buy earlier next year," I said impulsively. "I wish I had thought of this sooner, Milady. I'm so sorry."

"You've not been yourself for a while, Kitty," she said softly as she placed her ponytail head against my costumed shoulder.

"True," I smiled. "I'm sorry about that. And thanks for hanging in there with me."

"I knew I'd get you back eventually," she smiled back. "Vasily seems to have helped to speed up things."

I found myself nodding. "Both of us talked about what happened, finally," I explained. "I think we're through the worst of it, but there are still some unanswered questions at this point."

"Good," she replied. "He's not happy here, is he?"

"Not in the least. I don't think returning to Windeport is top of mind for him, though. Besides, he might hate his current posting, but he loves the California lifestyle." I paused. "Even if it seems to hate him."

"That's a bit harsh," she chuckled.

"Not really. He seems to have landed in the one town that he's incompatible with. Even Windeport was more open to him than what I've seen in Rancho Linda. It's horrible – like watching some time–capsule mid–eighties version of existence instead of now."

The lights flickered a bit, and then dimmed; Suzanne leaned in again for a kiss as the crowd quieted down for the keynote. "I hope you enjoy this," she enthused. "The speaker rarely does live events."

"I'm sure I will," I said, unsure if that was actually the truth.

"Liar," she laughed.

I have to admit to tuning out after the first several standing ovations; not being aware of pop culture had its downsides, and clearly not understanding the importance of the rotund and bearded man standing center stage was one of them. However, the concept artwork he was displaying was something even I could appreciate; I had taken an *Art of the Motion Picture* general education course in college, and the animation section had at the very least given me an understanding of the complexities of the artform. I wasn't quite clear whether what he was showing was pre–visualizations of something that was currently available, or something new.

After about ninety minutes of speaking, he settled in on a stool and allowed the audience some general questions. I was taken aback by the thoughtful queries coming out of people dressed as comic book characters; each was treated with respect by both the audience and the speaker. Quite a few had an incisive point to make, though the exact semantics of most of the questions were, of course, lost on me. Still, when the lights came up and we filed back out of the ballroom, I found myself caught up in the buoyant mood that had been generated by the session.

"That was quite remarkable," I said as we pushed out into the cold evening and found a spot to wait for Vasily.

"Season five is going to be amazing," she replied excitedly. "I can't believe how amazing those new transformations looked!"

"Yeah," I nodded, desperately hoping she wouldn't expect me to know more than I did.

Fortunately, Spider–Man sans his mask came strolling in our direction. "That was *insane*," Vasily gushed with a wide grin. "And I got his autograph just now!"

Suzanne's masked eyes widened in surprise and she suddenly snatched his badge. "My... God!" she breathed. "You have an *A–list pass?!*"

"Yeah," he said, his face flushing a bit. "I don't have many vices, but comics are one of them," he explained sheepishly. "The pass was a Christmas gift to myself, celebrating my new life here in California."

"Can I assume 'A–List' is better than our 'General Admission' badges?" I asked with a smile.

"Yes," Suzanne said as she let the pass drop through her fingers. "He gets exclusive access to the speakers and early entrance to the vendor hall. And, if I'm not mistaken, a certain number of autographs, too."

"Not to mention, uh, prime seating," he added quietly.

"Well, then," I said as I narrowed my masked eyes. "If you can afford *that*, the first round of drinks is on you."

He flushed a bit more. "Uh, would you believe I don't have any pockets in this costume?" he asked.

I groaned and turned to Suzanne. "Don't look at me," she laughed. "You're the only one with pockets."

Much later, the three of us were still sitting around a semi–circular table at the hotel bar. I'd finally managed to figure out how to sit without having the belt tail in an uncomfortable spot, but leaning my back against the baton had become painful. It sat on the table between the half–full wine glass of Suzanne's and the rum–and–coke I'd been drinking. Vasily's third mudslide was showing some condensation on the outside of the glass; I suspected it was the effects of the first two drinks that had me reach out a claw–tipped finger and try to catch a drop of condensation before it rolled to the napkin beneath Vasily's drink.

"What on Earth are you doing?" Suzanne asked.

"I'm a cat," I said somewhat dramatically, "and as such, I am fascinated by these rivulets of water."

"Admit it. You're just looking for a way to get to the milk in my drink," Vasily said, one booted foot over the edge of his chair.

"I don't like milk," I said.

"You just said you were a cat," Vasily reasoned. "My drink has milk. Q.E.D."

"Are you throwing Latin at me? In the middle of the night?"

"Technically it's early morning," he said with a yawn. "But yes. And I should really go."

"You can't leave in your condition," Suzanne said. "We've got a couch in our room. Stay the night."

"I'm fine," he said.

"How many of those have you had?" she asked him, pointedly.

"This is my third," he said, though his face scrunched. "I think."

"It's your fourth," she said as she waved to the waiter. "And since both of you have to work in the morning, I'm calling it a night for all of us."

"How many––?" I started to ask.

"Three. And this is my only glass of wine," she smiled. "Ladybug has to keep her wits about her, seeing as though she's running things."

"Hey!" Vasily cried. "I'm not even on your team! You can't boss around Spider–Man!"

"I can and I will. Come on, let's go before I smack you with my yo–yo."

"I love you, Ladybug," I said as we stood, rubbing my face against her shoulder like a cat.

"I know, Chat," she said sweetly. "I know."

Twenty-One

After a turn at the hotel's stellar breakfast buffet, and now knowing that Vasily was just a few blocks from us, I left the rental in the garage and drove with him over to the Rancho Linda High School. On his way out the door the prior afternoon, he'd gotten us back–to–back appointments to speak with the Principal, Guidance Counselor and the Tennis Coach. I sipped the Starbucks I'd picked up in the hotel as he navigated the craziness that was Southern California traffic.

"How can you possibly enjoy this?" I asked. "It's five lanes *everywhere*. Even on side streets."

He shrugged. "I grew up here, so it's not all that difficult. In fact, it was harder for me to get used to the smaller, more twisty roads back in Maine."

"That seems hard to believe."

"Not only that, but the smaller roads also feel more claustrophobic."

"I can actually see that," I nodded as I sipped again. "I still can't wrap my brain around how much real estate is dedicated to transportation out here."

"We love our cars in California," Vasily laughed. "How do you want to handle the morning?"

"Quickly," I chuckled. "Suzanne wants me back by early afternoon for some of the better panels at the convention. And some sort of dinner party."

"I'm going to that, too," he smiled. "We'll have to hustle, but I think we can make it by two? Assuming you still want to tackle the interviews with Mark and his partner."

"Yeah, I want to get that out of the way. Not sure there will be anything there, to be honest," I said, then smiled a bit craftily, "but I might be able to make Mark uncomfortable for a bit."

"I would sincerely appreciate that."

Vasily turned onto the boulevard that I recognized led toward the school; we'd driven the area the day before, slowly circumnavigating so I could eyeball the exact cellphone towers surrounding the school. We'd also poked in and out of the various obvious parking lot areas that Chase could have been in, but nothing jumped out at me.

As he slowed for a light a few blocks from the school, I found myself ruminating. "That gouge on the minivan. Did Chase sideswipe something? Or did someone nail him in one of those lots we perused yesterday?"

"I'd assumed the lab would be able to tell us if there is paint from another vehicle when they analyze it," Vasily said. "But to my eye, it looked like something was dragged the length of the minivan. Not quite keying, but something similar."

"Shopping cart?"

"I'd have to look again, but I think it's too high."

"Side mirror?"

"That's more likely. And would show damage if we can locate the vehicle."

Sipping my coffee, I continued. "It's lower than the mirrors on the van itself, so if it was a vehicle, it would have to be a smaller sedan or sports car."

"You might also consider one of those safety bollards, too."

"The what's?"

"You've seen them. Those barrier things that they put up along a sidewalk to keep cars from going through the front door of the shop."

I nodded. "Actually, that's a good thought," I said. "Did we see any of those on our travels yesterday?"

"Not that I recall," Vasily said.

I looked at the clock on my phone. "We are a little early – do me a favor, would you? Head over to that mall we found. But go around to the delivery docks."

"Sure," Vasily said as he shifted lanes and bypassed the turn toward the school. A few moments later, he was slowly turning into the shallow service alley behind a section of the mall. "I think this is within the cone of the cell coverage," he said.

"I'll cross check the map when we get back to the station," I said, my eyes scanning the alley as he slowly continued to drive. The space was just wide enough for a semi or a large delivery van; every few feet was a rollup door, and in one case we found a ramp down to a larger loading dock.

"What are you looking for?" Vasily asked.

"Just a hunch," I said. "When you said safety bollards, it got me thinking that the grocery store back home had them around the dumpster. In order to keep our senior citizens from running it over."

Vasily started. "Hot damn," he said. "Just like those, right?"

He pointed, and just ahead of us was a small dumpster surrounded by four concrete cylinders. All were painted in white, and there were parking spots on either side, presumably for staff working in the store.

"Pull up over there," I said.

Vasily pulled off as far as he could and put the SUV into park; I slid out of the passenger side and walked over to the first post. At about three feet tall, it had to be nearly the height of the long groove in the side of the minivan. It didn't hurt that it was painted white, which I was reasonably sure was the color inside the groove.

I pulled out my iPhone and started snapping photos. "This is about the right height. And there aren't that many along this portion of the service alley."

"There will be more around the entire perimeter," Vasily pointed out. "This mall has close to two hundred shops, so there have to be at least half as many dumpsters. And these posts aren't only around the trash receptacles."

"True, but it's worth tracking down how many are inside the cone of coverage from the cell towers." I looked up. "I'm still not discounting it was a car that nailed the minivan, but it doesn't hurt to have alternatives to look at."

"Agreed," Vasily said as he pulled out his phone. "I'll call the station and see if I can get some patrol officers to take paint samples of the posts at this mall and the small shopping center we drove through yesterday. It'll be a good test to see if Chief Gilbert truly will spare no expense at this point."

"I think too much is riding on this now," I replied. "He'll help."

I spent a few more minutes wandering the back of the shopping mall while Vasily requested our helpers. I found it intriguing how the front of the mall was impeccably themed and maintained, while the back was pure industrial, gritty and dirty with years of deliveries. The doors next to each loading area were marked with a suite number but nothing else, so it was impossible to know if I was standing behind a bookstore or a barber shop. What was not clear to me, yet, was why Chase would be back here.

I caught Vasily as he wrapped up his call. "Chase wasn't working a part time job, right?"

"No," he answered. "He had a pretty full schedule as an athlete. Why?"

"Nothing," I murmured. "Just another inconsistency."

"One of many," Vasily reminded me as we got back into the SUV.

He did a three-point turn and had us over to the school just a few minutes before our appointment with Janice Dolittle, the school's long-time principal. She was a tall, thin woman with white streaks in otherwise jet-black hair and was dressed in a conservative pantsuit that was nearly a standard uniform in education.

Waving us to two very hard plastic guest chairs, she smiled as we sat. "My secretary said you were here about Chase Cromwell?" she asked after we got through the niceties.

"Yes," I replied. "Just background, really. Trying to get a sense of him as a student."

She smiled, showing perfectly white teeth. "There's not much to tell,

I'm afraid. He wasn't the kind of kid that frequented those seats you are in," she chuckled. "I tend to only see them when there are disciplinary issues or other sorts of things the faculty can't handle on their own."

"He wasn't in any trouble of any kind, then?"

"No." She moved to her computer and tapped in something. "According to our records, not even a detention. He had nearly perfect attendance, too. That's actually rather extraordinary."

"He must have been up for some kind of award for that," I joked.

"Quite possibly," she laughed. "I can't remember the last time I did that certificate for someone. It's been years, I think."

"Student groups? Friends?" I prompted.

"Not really my area," she apologized. "The teachers would know more than I. If you want, I'll take you down to the staff lounge." She glanced at the round institutional clock on the wall. "We have a short fifteen-minute study hall/coffee break coming up. Just about everyone will be there."

"That would be brilliant," I said as we stood. "I'm sorry to have taken up your time."

"I'm sorry I couldn't tell you more."

"Vas," I started as we moved to the door. "Why don't we divide and conquer. You head to the lounge, and I'll take our next appointment."

"You were meeting with Ray next, right?" Janice asked.

"Chase's Guidance Counselor? Yes."

She chuckled. "He'll be in the lounge already, actually. Come this way."

We purposefully moved through hallways that looked much like the school I had attended back in Windeport. It seemed to me all schools had the same basic design: dull tile, duller colors and the faint smell of janitorial supplies. We appeared to be in the middle of a class change, though no one was in a particular hurry to get anywhere.

"The State mandated a fifteen-minute break in the morning and afternoon for the kids," Janice explained. "It's not exactly recess for the high school set, of course, but it does give the staff some downtime." She laughed. "Back in the old days it would have been nearly enough time to smoke one or two cigarettes before dealing with another hour of hormone-driven angst."

"Having lived through this myself as a teenager," I said as we came to a stop in front of a nondescript door, "I don't think you folks get paid enough."

"No," she laughed again as she pushed the door open in front of us. "We most certainly do not."

Twenty-Two

The staff lounge at Rancho Linda High School looked like a refugee camp, with the despondent scattered about the area in clutches of two or three, engaged in muted conversation. A few faces turned toward our arrival, then turned away; clearly, we were not viewed as being worth diverting precious moments of attention from their midmorning break. I wasn't sure I blamed them, for I was quite aware of the ever-growing demands being placed on the modern educator. I'd known a veteran of more than thirty years as a first-grade teacher that had retired on the spot when a parent demanded she potty train their kid.

Not particularly well appointed, there were multiple round tables in the center of the space; against one wall was a small kitchen counter loaded with *bric-à-brac* standard in any breakroom, from dishware draining on the sideboard to an industrial strength Keurig that looked like something picked up on markdown at the local warehouse store. A sad microwave from another era entirely was grinding its way through a cycle, the odor of singeing popcorn announcing that someone would be quite dissatisfied with the results of the operation.

A fridge from a manufacturer that hadn't existed in decades hummed loudly at the end of the counter, and a rear-end was all that was visible of Raymond Connolly as Principal Dolittle sailed in that direction. "Ray?"

There was a sudden movement, and then a muted curse as Ray smashed his head inside the fridge. Slowly, the torso withdrew from the

126

fridge and revealed a portly, balding man with a full beard. "Damn, Janice."

"Sorry, Ray," she said. "My apologies at startling you. These are the detectives that were going to meet with you?"

"Ah," Ray replied as he swapped his soda to the opposite hand and shook mine. "A pleasure, Mister...?"

I tried not to grimace at the cold, clammy embrace. "Sean Colbeth," I replied, nodding to Vasily. "This is my colleague, Vasily Korsokovach."

He released my hand and pumped Vasily's. "Nice to meet you," he said.

Vasily looked to me. "I'll rejoin you?" he asked.

"Absolutely," I smiled and turned back to Ray as Vasily wandered away with Janice. "Can we grab a table?"

"Sure, my stuff is over here. Let me get––damn–damn–*damn!*" he cried as smoke began to issue forth from the microwave.

For a man of his size, Ray moved fast and popped open the door to the microwave, flapping a file folder he'd been holding under his arm to get the plume of smoke to clear. Judging from the non–reaction of the other teachers in the room, this appeared to be a daily occurrence. I tried hard not to crinkle my nose as he brought the bag toward me and then guided me over to the table he'd indicated.

"Sorry," he apologized. "I always lose track of the time when I use that damn device. And it's old enough that sometimes it takes two minutes, sometimes thirty seconds." Pulling the bag open, more smoke belched out of the orifice. Frowning, he picked through it until he discovered a kernel safe enough to eat. "You're here about Chase?" he asked as he slid his files to the side and leaned on his arm.

"Yes."

"Good kid," he said as he sipped from his diet soda. "Straight–A student. Full ride scholarship to Berkeley – first from this school, by the way."

"I presume you met with him a few times?"

"Yeah, he was in my caseload. But nothing exciting, I'm afraid. Mostly planning out his coursework and then helping with college applications. Scheduling entrance exams, pulling together transcript information. Pretty standard stuff."

"No academic issues of any kind?"

"Nope. None. Perfect student," he said.

I examined my conversation mate, and noted he was idly running his finger along the edge of a file folder; his eyes were darting from my face to the clock just over my shoulder and then back again. Combined with how hasty his last answer had been to me, my radar went off.

The trick now would be to tease the actual information out of him.

"Can you tell me about his friends?" I asked impassively, watching him closely.

Ray looked down at his can of diet soda. "Not much," he said. "I know he had a few; he was well liked by his classmates, I think."

"You think? Or you know?"

"I don't interact with the students on a daily basis like the teachers do," he said as he looked up. "You might want to talk to them."

"We will," I said, "but I'd love to know your thoughts. You're a Guidance Counselor, after all; students are more likely to talk to you about non–academic issues than their teachers, right?"

Ray's eyes widened. "Whatever he told me would be confidential," he said, his voice quiet.

"So, he did tell you something, then?"

"That's not what I said!"

I lowered my voice. "Look, Counselor, I'm just trying to get a sense of who Chase was as a person. What his life was like – what he was like as a person. What motivated him to be a straight–A student." I leaned forward. "I never met him – I don't know him as you did. Anything you know – anything he might have shared with you – would help me to understand him better."

Ray blinked. "It's not really my place," he said, his voice even lower.

"I can assure you of my discretion, Counselor," I said softly. "Anything you might be able to tell me, no matter how insignificant it might seem to you, could be important to my investigation."

"I thought it was an accident?" he asked.

"We're just being thorough," I smiled, careful with my nondenial.

Ray looked at me for a long moment, then down to his soda, then back to me. "Chase... Chase was troubled."

"In what way?"

Ray sighed. "This is between us?"

"As much as it can be," I nodded.

He looked away and then back again. "Kids his age are often conflicted for many reasons. They worry about pleasing their parents, whether it means going to the school they want them to attend or ensuring they are scoring top marks." He sipped his soda. "Even though they'd rather go to another school, or hate the coursework they are engaged in."

"I can understand that."

"Then there are other issues that are endemic to teens. Identity issues," he said. "I didn't know all of it, but from what Chase told me over the course of our meetings this year, he was really struggling with something very personal. And felt like he wasn't getting any support at home."

I nodded. "Identity issues of what sort?"

"I'm not sure," he said honestly. "He did have a small circle of friends, very small for someone like him, actually. The teachers might know more than I do – the only reason I know what little I do is that I recommended talking to a peer about his concerns. He said he would but didn't have many people to turn to."

"It seems unusual that a star athlete wouldn't have a large cadre of acquaintances."

Ray smiled for the first time. "As much as I would like to argue that is an unfair stereotype, it's actually generally accurate. But not for Chase. He was a bit of an outlier."

"Did you suspect any sort of family issues, then? Abuse? That sort of thing?"

"No," he said thoughtfully. "If anything, maybe something along the lines of bullying. But I have no firm evidence, despite pressing Chase on it as much as I could." He sighed as a bell rang out in the distance. "I have to get to my next appointment," he apologized as he tidied up the files and stood. "But Chase was a good kid, Detective. Whatever his issues were, they didn't affect his career here at the school in any negative way."

I shook his hand. "Thank you for your candor," I said. "You've been helpful."

"Have I?" he said quizzically. "I guess that's good," he smiled as he quickly escaped from me.

I watched him press through the door and tried not to laugh. It wasn't the first time someone had scurried away from the authorities. I suspected I would be chatting with him again. Turning, I saw Vasily heading toward me.

"That was interesting," he said as he closed his notebook. "You?"

"Plenty to think about," I nodded. "Learn anything?"

"Quite a bit," he said. "I'd compare notes, but we're to meet with the Tennis Coach in a few minutes. He's waiting for us out at the courts."

"All right," I smiled. "Lead the way."

Twenty-Three

Dalton Ramsfeld met us just outside of a set of four tennis courts adjacent to the gymnasium for the high school. He was about what I expected: lean, well-built, and gregarious, tanned from being outside with sun streaks in his brown hair. He was dressed in shorts and a logoed t–shirt which, when I examined it more closely, was of the same style and cut as what Chase had been wearing at the time of his demise.

"Coach?" I said as I held out my hand. "Chief Colbeth, Detective Korsokovach."

"Hey," he smiled as he shook our hands. "Shame about Chase."

My eyebrows went up, for he was the first person who had expressed any sort of emotion over Chase. "How long had you been his coach?"

"A while," he smiled. "I've been the school coach for years, but also do private lessons for younger kids. To be honest, I use it as a pipeline for the school. Chase came to me at age seven."

"Was he some sort of tennis prodigy?" Vasily asked.

I nodded at the line of thought, for that was actually how both of us had become Olympic swimmers. I'd been in the pool from the age of five; I was pretty sure Vasily had taken his first backstroke at age six. We'd often joked that our blood was eight percent chlorine. Looking at Dalton reminded me of that first swim coach I'd had myself; unlike Chase, I'd been through a succession of them as I'd aged through the program.

"Yes," Dalton said without hesitation. "That kid could zero in on the ball at seven and was acing his competition at twelve with serves close to seventy miles an hour. I'd never seen anything like it. Tennis was just second nature to Chase." He sighed as he started to take us down a short pathway to a set of bleachers outside of one of the courts. "I've done this for more than twenty years now, guys, and I truly have never seen a talent such as his. Simply amazing."

We took seats on a row above where Dalton perched on the lowest level. "I take it he must have had some statewide accolades," I said.

"He was consistently in the top ten of players in his division. It was why he was so heavily recruited – again, something I'd not seen in my years here as a coach." He shook his head again. "I can't believe he's gone," he added softly. "I still expect to see him turn up at practice each day. He was as regular as clockwork."

"Is that unusual?" Vasily asked.

"For teenagers? Oh my *God*, yes." He pulled a pack of gum out of his pocket and offered us each a piece before grabbing one himself. As he tore back the foil, he nodded again – a mannerism that I would grow tired of if I'd had to work with him daily. "I have a hard time keeping kids interested in tennis, to be honest. It's not as sexy as other sports like football; soccer is kind of the same way." He laughed. "The World Cup does wonders for them, actually. And Chase's quiet success brought us more attention than normal. His dedication to the team – and to the sport – attracted a following, and to be honest, I am worried about keeping up the enthusiasm."

"He was well–liked by his teammates, then?"

"No question," he said as he put the foil into his pocket. "He was voted captain his junior and senior years. I expected he'd earn his letter this year for sure."

Mindful of what Ray had said to me, I ventured into new territory. "Did you see any changes in him recently? Or in the last few months?"

Dalton paused. "How do you mean? Physical? Or Mental?"

I raised an eyebrow. "Either I suppose."

Dalton paused again. "Well, he'd been a gym rat for years... but now that I think about it, he did seem to bulk up a bit more this winter than I expected." He shrugged. "I assumed he'd had a growth spurt and added some muscle in the process. It happens. We have some football players that look far older than eighteen, I can assure you."

That made me smile. "How about mental?"

"That's not really my area of expertise," he laughed nervously. "I mean, I have to do a fair amount of sports psychology to keep the team motivated of course. But as to personal issues?" He shrugged. "To be honest, any of the kids could have broken up with their girlfriends – or boyfriends, for that matter – and I wouldn't have a clue."

Vasily took the opening. "Boyfriends?" he ventured carefully.

Dalton rolled his eyes. "It's a brave new world, Detective. I might coach the men's team, but I have two trans kids, one questioning and one openly gay. They didn't teach me how to handle those dynamics in my Master's program, I can assure you."

"You seem to have a pretty good sense of your team," Vasily observed. "Did the players self–identify?"

Dalton flushed slightly. "Well... not really. But kids are far more open than they used to be. And we've all been trained in how to work with kids from all backgrounds."

"Where did Chase fall in that spectrum?" I asked.

Dalton flushed more. "I... well, to be honest, I think he had a girl-friend. Not that it means anything these days." He looked away. "Bob-bie? I think that was her name. He had a photo of her in his locker; I found it when I cleaned it out for his parents."

I looked at Vasily, and raised an eyebrow. He made a note in his book.

"And how did Chase interact with such a diverse group?"

Dalton laughed. "Well, I would think. They wouldn't have elected him captain unless he had their back, right?"

I shot another look at Vasily, who nodded slightly. "Good point. Thank you for your time, Coach. If you happen to think of anything else, please call us at this number," I said as Vasily handed him his card.

"I will," Dalton said. "Terrible loss," he said softly. "Just terrible."

Twenty-Four

Vasily had taken us to the nearest Starbucks, and though we were cozily ensconced around a small table on the open–air patio, it had none of the ambiance of Calista's Bakery back in Windeport. The coffee was good, of course, but the pastries definitely left a lot to be desired. I took solace in the amazing view instead, for it was perched in another of the surprising number of small hills that were Rancho Linda. Blue skies appeared to be fairly normal for Southern California, even in the winter, and I was starting to understand why people flocked to the area.

I tried hard not to start liking it.

Sipping my coffee and picking at what I had been told was a blueberry muffin, I pondered the information we had gathered so far. "Let me see if I have a good summary of what is likely in your notes," I said. "Everyone liked Chase. He had no enemies, was a perfect student and extraordinary athlete."

"And... he had a girlfriend," Vasily pointed out. "Something his parents haven't mentioned."

"Once we start digging through his social media, we are bound to find her," I said. "That could be why Adele was so uncomfortable. And why the photos from the phone had been deleted."

"True."

"So, what did we actually learn?"

"He's a perfect kid," Vasily said.

I poked at a blueberry with my fork; it was rubbery. Blueberries weren't supposed to be rubbery. "Was he? Or was that what he wanted people to see?"

"That's a rather cynical view," Vasily said.

"It is. But I have rarely found people I investigate are always on the up–and–up." I looked up at Vasily. "If we operate under the assumption that Chase did not die by his own hand, that requires us to consider just what could bring someone to kill him. And that requires us to con-template that he's not quite as squeaky clean as everyone would have us believe."

Vasily sipped his coffee. "Wow. Someone woke up on the wrong side of the bed this morning."

"Not really. It's Investigation 101. You know that."

"I do," he smiled. "It just sounds different hearing it from you for some reason." He looked over my shoulder. "Maybe it's the location."

"Or maybe you ignored my teachings back in Maine, grasshopper."

Vasily's eyes snapped to mine. "Oh no," he smiled slyly. "I observed every one of them. Completely."

I rolled my eyes. "That'll teach me."

"And those tight polo shirts—"

"Vas," I said, rolling my eyes again. "Please."

"Sorry. But can you blame me?" he laughed.

I glared at him. "*Any*way," I continued, "I haven't heard anything yet that makes any sense as a motive for why someone might kill him. I feel as though we have a ton of interesting threads, but the vast majority of them can be easily explained as being a pretty typical teenager, albeit one with superior skills in tennis."

"And academics," Vasily said.

"Academics..." I said, tapping my fork's tines against the faux wood surface of the table. "Did I tell you about the documents I found on his laptop?"

"No."

"It was odd. I was looking through the folders and found what I pre-sumed was work he had done for his classes; I opened a few, and found that in addition to the other talents we already know about, he seems to be a pretty decent writer for his age."

"Not unusual, given who his father is."

"True." I sipped my coffee. "Then there was another folder, and there were hundreds of documents in it – but they were actually the *same* document, written just differently enough that it would be hard to know they had been done by the same author." I smiled slightly. "I read more than I intended, and even though Chase did an excellent job of mixing it up a little in each version, I could tell that they were all his work."

Vasily stared at me. "Why would he have those?" he asked before he caught himself. "Hang on, was he a one–person term paper mill?"

I nodded. "I think so, yes. And I'm willing to bet he wrote each version just differently enough that they wouldn't be caught by the anti–plagiarism software so common these days. Or a harried teacher who feels like the paper is familiar but can't place it."

"That's clever," Vasily said. "But he's a teenager – I can't imagine I'd be able to find any financials that would prove he was receiving pay-ment for his services."

"True. And I doubt he was turning it over to his parents for deposit either."

Vasily looked thoughtful. "There are other forms of payment besides cash, Sean," he said slowly. "I'm not suggestion anything in particular, but maybe he was getting paid in kind."

I nodded. "Possible, but we'll have to prove he was a document mill in the first place."

"Send me the documents and I'll head back to the school and shop them around to his teachers," Vasily said. "I can do the legwork while you peruse his social media."

"Yeah," I said as I finished the last of my coffee. "Maybe our new friends in the crime lab will have something for us today, too."

"I tried to get us to the top of the queue," Vasily said. "But we share time with the other departments in the County. I don't want to get your hopes up; it could be tomorrow at the earliest."

I smiled. "That would free up my afternoon, then," I laughed. "And make Suzanne very happy."

Vasily's phone buzzed and he angled it up to read. "Ah. Our intrepid investigators are free and ready to speak to us," he said as he tapped out a reply. "Are you ready to meet them?"

"As ready as I'll ever be. Let's get this over with."

Mark Friedman and his partner of the moment, Milorad Guernsey, were waiting for us in the same conference room where we'd talked to Mike the day before. The Chief was apparently meeting with *his* boss, conveniently ensuring he would be out of the office when we met with the troublesome detective.

Vasily and I had taken the seats against the windows, forcing Mark and Miles to look into the slight glare of the noontime sun. It was a minor irritant, to be sure, but I wanted to use every trick available to me to ensure I could root out the truth. "Gentleman," I smiled as we all sat. "Thanks for taking the time to talk to me. I only have a few questions about the Chase Cromwell case."

"Case?" Mark snorted. "What case? It was an accident. A terrible, cruel, accident."

"Indeed," I said with a smile. "What led you to determine it was an accident?"

"I wasn't the investigator," he said as he crossed his arms, subtly flexing his biceps as he did. I noted he had made an effort to not look at Vasily.

"Really? I understood that you started the initial work on the investigation," I said, feigning a puzzled expression. "Was I misinformed?"

"No," Miles said. "We—"

"Yes," Mark snapped, glaring at his partner. "We had no part in the investigation short of being interviewed after the fact."

"But you were the first car on the scene?"

"Well, technically."

"I see. So, walk me through that."

"There's not much to walk through," Mark said. "We drove through multiple lots, looking for a civilian in distress. We really had no idea what exactly we were looking for, so it was hard to know what to expect."

"You didn't see anything out of the ordinary, then?"

"No. Nothing."

"Was the minivan in the parking lot when you drove through it?"

"It must have been," Mark said. "But like I said, we had no idea *what* we were looking for. It could have been a grandmother who'd tripped over a dog. Or a bicyclist that had been hit by a truck."

"I see your point," I said pleasantly, before turning to Miles. "And did you see the minivan?"

"No," he said firmly.

Mark looked at him. "Maybe you did," he said, a slight edge to his voice.

"No, Mark," Miles said just as firmly. "That van was memorable. I'm certain it wasn't there when we drove through."

"You didn't mention that when I spoke with you initially," Vasily interjected. "Why?"

Miles looked at Mark. "I... didn't think it was important at the time, to be honest," he said, and it had the ring of truth to my ear. "After I heard Chief Colbeth had been brought in, though, I've been thinking about it a bit more. The van wasn't there when Mark and I drove through. That gash on the side makes it rather recognizable."

Mark glared. "Miles, that van was there. You have no way to know either way."

"Maybe, maybe not," Miles said. "But I'm thinking not."

"You're mistaken," Mark said, and even I could hear the threatening undercurrent. "The kid called from that lot!"

"I don't think so," I replied evenly. "We are reasonably sure his phone wouldn't have been able to connect to a cell tower from that location."

Mark stared at me. "Say... say what?"

"Poor cell coverage," Vasily said with a trace of a smile. "I'm sure you noticed when you did your survey of the lot." He paused a beat, pencil hovering over his notebook. "Oh, wait, I see here that you were in a rush to leave the scene." He looked up again. "Maybe you didn't follow protocol after all."

"We did," Mark said hotly. "Miles will back me up on that, at least."

"Milorad?" I asked.

A wry smile came to the younger detective's face. "Mark felt strongly there wasn't much to be gained by continuing to search. I objected, but as the junior officer was overruled. I did, however, lodge a complaint with Dispatch." He looked sideways at his partner. "Just in case this ever came up."

"Damn you, Miles," Mark said. "You'll never—"

"I'd be careful, Detective," I said. "I'm duty bound to report this conversation to your superior. If it were to be construed that you threatened a fellow officer – in front of a superior officer, no less – well, I'm not certain I'd want that smudge on my personal file, to be honest."

Mark fell silent.

"Were you the initial investigator on the case?"

"It was never a case," he said sullenly.

"Call it what you wish, then. Were you in charge?"

"I was the first to run the initial data gathering, yes," he said reluctantly. "I – we – had another case already in progress, so I handed it off to Detective Korsokovach."

"I see. And what did you find during your initial inquiries?"

"There was nothing to *find*," Mark replied.

"Walk me through what little you did, then," I said neutrally, getting no pleasure in seeing him tense at my choice of words.

"Once the father found the minivan, he called 9–1–1 and we happened to also be the closest car. Dispatch sent us back to the school; we found the father beside the minivan, apoplectic as any parent would be."

I nodded. "And?"

"And – nothing! We called in the paramedics even though it was fairly obvious the kid had expired. As I expected, they called it within a few moments of arriving. The coroner was right behind them."

"You followed procedure, of course."

"Yes, damn it," he said. "Even though there was no point. We took photos, bagged everything we could find and took statements. But at the end of the day, it was an accident." He refolded his arms again and pressed his lips into a thin line. "I hate to break it to wunderkind and you; it was an accident. A terrible, tragic and highly unusual one to be sure, but it *was* an accident."

"I see." I looked to Vasily. "One last question."

"Okay."

"The father called it in the third time?"

"Yes," Milorad answered. "At least, that's what Dispatch told me. I took the call."

"Where, exactly, did you meet up with the father."

Miles looked confused. "In the parking lot, just as Mark said. Beside the minivan."

"All right," I smiled. "Thank you."

"That's it?" Mark said.

"From me," I smiled wider. "The disciplinary board, however, will likely have some questions for you."

Mark stared at me. "For what?"

"You appear to have a pattern of badgering fellow officers, Detective. I believe that is a violation of the standards and practices of the department." I stood up as a dismissal. "You might want to schedule an appointment with your union rep."

Mark looked between me and Vasily. "Is this some sort of retribution?" he asked, before turning his ire on Vasily. "So, help me, if you are trying to take me down—"

"And there's another data point for the committee," I interrupted. "Thank you, Detective."

Fuming, Mark stood up hard enough that his chair flew backward and tipped over. He ignored it as he moved through the doorway; Miles paused and turned back with a half-smile. "Is he going to be written up?" he asked.

"Yes," I nodded. "I've seen enough that another investigation is warranted, I think."

"Good," Milorad said. "Thank you," he said quietly as he slipped out himself.

Vasily flipped his notebook closed as we packed up the files we'd had as props. "Well, that didn't get us much, did it?"

I smiled at my friend. "Oh, it netted us another clue, Vas."

He stared at me. "Clue? What clue?"

I chuckled. "I would now like to turn our attention to the curious case of the father who appears to have made a cell phone call from a dead zone at the school parking lot."

Vasily blinked. "I'll get the car."

Twenty-Five

Vasily took the helm once more while I enabled the hotspot on my phone and logged into my laptop; before we spoke with Parker Cromwell a second time, I wanted to confirm a hunch that had been in the back of my head nearly from the moment Mark made his fatal mistake during the interview. To my surprise, we appeared to be moving through an exceptional area of cellular data access. "The internet is pretty snappy through here," I said appreciatively. "You might need to slow down so I can savor this."

He laughed. "We're passing through the high end of town at the moment. Unlike the school, I would expect the coverage to be pretty solid."

"That it is," I murmured as I juggled the dongle that connected the USB to the Mac. It took a moment, but I was able to quickly pull up the metadata from the 9–1–1 call Parker had made. While it looked familiar, I needed to plug it into my proprietary cellphone software to confirm my suspicion. "Identical cone," I said as I poked around the interactive map. "This confirms Parker was in the same general vicinity as where his son's cell made it's calls."

"Which we know couldn't have been in the school parking lot," Vasily added. "Do you think he's the one that moved the van?"

"Maybe," I nodded. "Though it's pretty risky to have called 9–1–1 and then relocated before the cops found him."

"He could have made the call while he was driving," Vasily pointed out. "I'll listen to the audio of his call with the 9–1–1 operator and see if I divine anything."

"Good, for I don't expect to get anything out of Parker this time around."

As it turns out, I was right about that one aspect, but for the wrong reason. No one answered the door when we rang the bell at the McMansion for the Cromwell's, which seemed extraordinary given that we'd been led to believe Adele was more or less housebound.

"Out for a spin?" I surmised. "It probably means nothing, as they wouldn't have been expecting us."

"True," Vasily said pensively. "I could be wrong, but it felt like Parker worked from home. And Adele was usually with him."

"Give them a call," I said as we started back down the stone steps to the circular drive. "See if we can make another appointment."

Vasily was one step ahead of me and was already dialing the number. He frowned as he left a voicemail. "Unusual. I've never had trouble getting ahold of him."

I paused in front of the three–car garage. "Maybe they just went grocery shopping?" I asked.

"Maybe."

"Call again."

He dialed once more and left a second message, then hung up. "It's a bit out of character for them to be out and about," he frowned. "But like you said, it probably means nothing."

"We'll try them again tonight," I said as we moved back to the SUV. "I've got plenty to do still before we meet up with Suzanne this afternoon."

"Same," Vas agreed as we pulled out of the parking lot. "Let me pick up my gear at the station and then we can work out of your mini–headquarters at the hotel."

"As long as I get another cup of coffee before we go up," I laughed.

"You and your coffee," he said, shaking his head.

We made reasonably good time and got back to the hotel a smidge after one. Suzanne met us in the lobby bar, having had the presence of mind to order us lunch. "I know you have work to do," she smiled as she kissed me, "so I'll eat and get out of your hair. Besides, there's a panel at two–thirty I need to get into line for fairly soon if I want to get a seat."

"Is that the retrospective on Miyazaki?" Vasily asked.

"Yes," Suzanne answered. "Are you a fan as well?"

"Huge," he said. "*Howl's Flying Castle* is nearly my favorite, but I think *Kiki's Delivery Service* edges it slightly. The panel was one I'd circled when I got my ticket. Now, though…" he trailed off with a trace of sadness, his eyes darting to the stack of files he'd grabbed.

"Go," I said. "It'll give me time to go through the social media sites. Then I'll meet you for the dinner gala at – what time?"

"It's at five, love," Suzanne smiled. "But we'll be back before that to get you into costume."

I rolled my eyes. "Again? I thought it was just the one night!"

"It's a comic convention," she laughed. "By rights I should be back into my costume already."

I looked to Vasily. "She's right. I should warn you, it's likely to be a long weekend if you don't reconcile yourself to the notion that you'll be Chat Noir from Friday night to Monday morning."

"You're not actually thinking of wearing that Spider–Man costume the entire time, are you?"

"No," he answered with a smile.

"Good," I said as I turned triumphantly toward Suzanne. "See? Even Vasily–––"

"I have three other costumes," he interrupted. "I can be someone different each day."

My head swung around. "You're not very helpful, you know that?"

"I do," he laughed as he balled up his napkin and stood to leave with Suzanne. "Come on," he said. "I might be able to cut in line with my VIP pass and get *both* of us a good seat."

"Stop trying to curry favor with my girlfriend," I accused good naturedly.

"I can't hear you," he laughed as they headed down the hallway that connected to the convention center.

I signed the check and headed back toward the room; much as before, I found myself pulling back the curtain on the wide windows looking down on the park–like area outside the hotel, watching the increased volume of costumed convention goers wandering back and forth. There was a significant part of me looking forward to donning the mask, ears and tail again, I found myself realizing as I gazed on view. Much like the character I was supposed to be portraying, I had begun to discover the freeing qualities of living behind a mask, of being someone else for a while without fear of discovery. It was an oddly appealing aphrodisiac of sorts, and as I watched the people below, I quite suddenly realized I understood their attraction to the entire enterprise.

For the second time since arriving with Suzanne, I realized how good an idea it had been to suggest attending the convention. Not just for her – that part was a given, of course. Despite myself, I could feel a part of me giving in to the fantasy; if not completely, for a short while as an escape from what we had gone through back in Windeport. It felt like some kind of healing, if I were being honest with myself, though *why* it waited to begin until I was thousands of miles from home and embroiled in a messy investigation was beyond me.

No – no, that wasn't quite right. I *did* know why, for I was once again surrounded by people I cared about, deeply, and who cared about *me* as well – each in their own way. I'd needed both of them, working in quasi–tandem, to pull me out of whatever funk I had been in since Vasily had left. What worried me was the next act, though... what would happen when we ultimately had to pack up and return to Maine.

I shoved that thought aside as I let the curtain fall from my fingers. Much like Scarlett O'Hara, I decided it could wait for another day. Even I was capable of self–denial and self–delusion, apparently.

Pulling on a pair of rubber gloves once more, I slid Chase's computer out of evidence bag and turned the MacBook Air back in. This time I pulled up his web browser of choice and first looked through its history. Unsurprisingly, it had been scrubbed much like the photos had been earlier; using the password vault system Adele had provided access to, though, I was able to log back into the main profile he'd used and quickly found the last few *years* of internet browsing available from the cloud.

Once more, the attempt to scrub the computer felt very much like it had been done by a novice, or someone with a very limited understanding of how cloud–connected systems worked. My curiosity was also piqued by *why* someone was so concerned about what someone might find on Chase's computer. Clearly there was something buried here that we were not supposed to see.

There was nearly too much material to go through without some of the better AI–driven tools we had access to normally, so I decided to brute force it a bit with entries for the past few weeks. It was a bit of a gamble, but my gut told me whatever might have happened would have taken place fairly close to Chase's death. If nothing looked promising, I'd go back further, though my heart sank at how much needed to be reviewed. Unless I got really lucky, the chances of me reading his social media posts that afternoon looked grim.

An hour flew by as I reviewed searches he had done, websites he had poked through and recent bookmarks that had been added to his browser. Most seemed related to being an average teen – though to my surprise, there was no trace of anything remotely pornographic. Multiple reports out of the FBI and other respected investigative research groups I subscribed to generally indicated that kids Chase's age spent between one and fifteen percent of their time on such sites, mostly as a replacement for the dearth of sex education programs nationwide. The lack of *anything* at all seemed extraordinary to the extreme, meaning he had either done an amazing job of covering his tracks, or he was truly the exceptional kid everyone had been telling us he was.

I couldn't understand why I was having such trouble accepting he was the perfect example of a teenager. Could I be getting more cynical the longer I was in this job? I was introspective enough to think not, and I generally found my finely–honed instincts rarely led me astray. And yet, nothing stood out to me from what I'd seen so far.

Sitting back, I rubbed my eyes and realized another hour had flashed past with little notice; according to the clock on the menu bar, Vasily and Suzanne would be returning soon. I decided to pause my research and start the laborious process of getting into my costume with the hope I'd be out of the way when Suzanne arrived, for she tended to need every square inch of the bathroom in order to transform herself into Ladybug. I ran through the shower at warp speed and managed to squeeze into the form–fitting costume all by myself; I was just fastening the belt tail about my waist when the lock to the door chirped, followed by the entrance of Suzanne and Vasily.

"Hey beautiful," I purred, partially in character as I kissed her upon entry.

"Kitty," she smiled. "You managed well without us," she observed appreciatively.

"All but the wig, ears and mask," I replied. "Those are well beyond my humble abilities."

"Sit back down and I'll do the honors," Vasily offered.

"Thanks," I said. "How was the panel?" I asked as I settled in.

"Amazing," Suzanne called out from the bathroom.

I could hear the water running and then the shower starting so I twisted up to Vasily. "Really?"

"Yes," he said, "and face forward, please," he added as he slipped the wig and attached ears over my unruly curls. "They had some snippets from his last film on offer, and then some of the voice talent was here discussing their time working with Miyazaki." I heard him laugh as he pinned the wig. "I scored points with your girlfriend. My VIP pass got us in the fourth row."

"I'm glad I suggested you go with her, then," I said. "Thanks."

"My pleasure," he said. "Okay, turn around and close your eyes."

Dutifully, I flipped around in the chair and squeezed my eyes shut. A moment later, I felt him begin to brush on the eye black. "This dinner tonight – what should I expect?"

He chuckled again. "The *gala*," he corrected, "is one of the highlights of the weekend. Think of it as a well-attended masked ball, with the wildest cast of characters every assembled. There will be massive buffets of food, music, and some dancing if you are up for it."

"I have two left feet," I groaned.

"Paws."

"Sorry?"

"Stay in character," he laughed. "Two left *paws*."

"I am doomed," I frowned.

"You'll be surprised how much you will enjoy it, I think…" he trailed off.

I snuck open an eye, recognizing he'd had an epiphany. "What?"

"Is that Chase's browsing history?"

I swiveled around and opened the other blackened eye. "Yeah," I said. "Someone tried to delete it, but I pulled everything back from the cloud, much like the photos that I've not had time to go through." I turned back toward him, feeling the hair and ears shift slightly as I did. "Why?"

He pointed to an entry on the list. "That's the store we were behind today. The one with the dumpster you were checking out."

I turned back, eyes widening. "*The Alternative Way*," I read. "Sounds like a beatnik coffeeshop."

"It's more like a bookstore with a coffeeshop inside," Vasily said, though his voice was strained.

Turning once more, I saw his expression. "They aren't selling books about the Vegan lifestyle, are they?"

"No," he said. "They most certainly are not."

Twenty-Six

A s I discovered the following morning, *The Alternative Way* catered to the LGBTQ community of Rancho Linda. Driving over from Anaheim, Vasily filled me in. "There are few places in this particular county that are friendly for that clientele," he said. "The counties around us are more open and accommodating, but *this* county happens to be the last bastion of what we euphemistically refer to as 'traditional mores.'"

"That seems to align with the treatment you've received at the department," I observed. "I take it there isn't a footnote on the town's Chamber of Commerce website that might have clued you in to this close–mindedness before you arrived?"

"No," he chuckled. "I'm considering starting my own website, though."

"You've been to this bookstore, then?"

"A few times," he allowed, his face flaming slightly. "They attract a well–heeled crowd, especially on the evenings they do live music. Usually Friday and Saturday."

"Adults, though?"

"Generally," he replied. "At least, the concerts are usually over twenty–one. They serve alcohol at them." He glanced at me. "You still have a bit of eye black on your left lid."

"Damn," I said as I pulled down the visor and tried to rub away the last vestiges of my costume. Vasily hadn't been wrong; the party had been fantastic and had lasted well into the early hours of the morning. I'd crashed beside Suzanne close to three only to wake a few hours later, still in my Chat costume. She'd been sound asleep still and therefore unavailable to help with my makeup removal. Clearly old–fashioned soap and water didn't do the job.

"At the risk of sounding like a Neanderthal," I said as I realized I was simply smearing the eye black further, "is there any reason other than the obvious that Chase would be visiting this establishment?"

Vasily chuckled. "They have the best coffee in town," he said. "And it's the closest place to the school to get a cup." He shrugged. "The most obvious explanation might be the best."

I slid my dark sunglasses on, resigned that I'd have to act like a movie star until I could correctly get the smudge fixed. "I'm happy to go with that," I concurred. "I wonder, though, if someone else read into it."

"You mean like the person who wiped out his browsing history?" Vasily said. "I could see that. In this day and age, though, it's not the same level of slur that it once was. Hell, if Chase *had* been gay, he might have had an even *better* chance of landing a scholarship."

"Based on what we know about Chase," I said as we turned into the parking lot of the mall, "he strikes me as the kind of kid who would have announced it to the world – and without compunction."

"I agree," Vasily said. "That doesn't mean, though, that others might have a vested interest in him being on one side of the fence or the other."

"And being upset, you think, if he chose poorly?" I nodded. "I've seen motives over less. You know what this means, right?"

"Yeah," he said grimly. "Talking to his peers." He pulled into a spot and put the SUV into park. "I hate interviewing teens."

"Me, too. I might be able to pare it down a bit though after I tackle his social media. Someone is bound to stick out there."

"That's your next task after this?" he asked as we exited the vehicle and started toward the entrance to the mall.

"I've delayed long enough," I groaned.

Very few of the big anchor stores were open at that early hour, but the food court and a bunch of smaller stores appeared to be doing brisk business. Based on the convoluted internal layout of the mall, it turned out to be a rather long walk to *The Alternative Way*; the smell of freshly brewed coffee, though, hit my nose as we rounded a final curve in the corridor and entered the bookstore. If I hadn't looked carefully at the titles, I'd have assumed the store was a very ordinary shop, with aisles of well stocked bookshelves carefully organized by genre and author.

The store was well lit and nicely carpeted, and was surprisingly busy, though most of the patrons were in line for the barista at the rear of the space. Soft jazz music was playing over the loudspeakers, and there was an intimate performance area in the far corner surrounded by a cozy arrangement of small round tables and a ring of couches. I felt myself relaxing, which I knew was the carefully orchestrated idea.

A pleasantly plump woman with purple hair and long, half–moon earrings greeted us. "Howdy," she smiled, her hands clasped behind her blue apron. "Here for coffee, a good read or both?"

"Information, originally," I replied, "but the coffee smells divine."

"We're serving Mexican Organic today," she beamed. "My partner has a connection in Sonora who farms it responsibly. We don't have it in stock often, so I highly recommend trying a cup." She smiled wider. "Or two."

"I will," I said.

"What kind of information are you looking for?" she asked.

"We're looking into the death of a local high school student," Vasily explained. "You might have heard about it on the news?"

"Chase Cromwell?" she shook her head. "Yes, and we knew him, too. Tragic."

My eyes widened. "You... knew him?"

"Of course," she said. "He is – was," she corrected sadly, "a volunteer with our chapter of the Southern California HIV/AIDS Foundation. Had been for years. I'm the co–chair at the moment, so I've been host-ing the meetings here in the store before we open for the day. Usually twice a month on Saturdays."

"Was Chase here that day?"

"The day he died?" she asked, and considered me for a long moment. "Yeah, I believe he was." She held out her hand. "I'm Anne."

"Sean," I smiled. "And this is my colleague, Vasily."

Anne smiled. "Vasily is a regular, Sean," she laughed. "He must have mentioned that."

"He did," I said, turning a wry smile on my slightly-flustered friend. "Not in so many words."

"Were you out late last night, Sean?" Anne chuckled. "We don't normally get the Hollywood treatment here."

It was my turn to feel my face flame slightly. Sliding off my sunglasses, I smiled a bit sheepishly. "I'm something of a novice at makeup," I said figuring the truth was the best option. "My girlfriend and I have been moonlighting at the comic convention in Anaheim. And yes, I was out late last night, late enough that I pretty much crashed as soon as we got back to the hotel room. I managed to scrub out most of it, but Vasily pointed out I'd missed a spot."

Anne laughed and tugged me toward a corner of a store. "I'm sure you have more questions, but let's take care of that faux black eye first, shall we? As it turns out, we happen to be well equipped in that department."

"Sorry?" I asked quizzically as she slid open a pocket door and took me into what looked like a stock room. "I thought this was a bookstore, not a cosmetic shop?"

"What we are is a safe, affirming space," she continued as she pulled me down a short hallway. Opening a wood-paneled door, she led me into what appeared to be the sort of makeup/green room setup you'd see actors or celebrities use, complete with a sizable mirror surrounded by lit bulbs. "Have a seat," she said as she indicated a foldable director's chair set center beneath the mirror and lights.

"Okay," I said, shooting a worried glance at Vasily.

"One second... here we are," she said triumphantly as she produced a small round container of cold cream. "Close your eyes. This will take but a moment."

I did as instructed and felt her begin to apply the emulsion to my face. "I'm fairly new at – what is it called, Vasily?"

"Cosplay, Chief."

"Right," I smiled. "My girlfriend has been slowly showing me the ropes."

"We do something similar here, in conjunction with another group," Anne said as she deftly worked the material over me. "There are a lot of teens, much like Chase, who are trying to find their way forward."

"I'm not sure I understand," I said.

I heard Anne run some water and then felt a warm washcloth against my skin. "Not everyone understands who or what they are, Sean," Anne said simply. "Much like the work we do with the Foundation, we have a few mornings each week set aside to create a safe space for people of all ages to discover themselves. And, in some cases, learn how to express that."

A light bulb went off. "You're talking about identity, aren't you?" I asked. "In all forms?"

"Yes," she said. "As Vas can probably tell you, this particular part of the county isn't very accommodating to people not of the perceived 'normal' stripe. We're the only spot currently available for folks to hang out and be themselves. No questions asked." She laughed. "We let everyone *else* in during normal business hours."

I felt myself smile again. "You're a social worker, aren't you?"

"Guilty as charged," she chuckled. "That's where I met my partner, Zoe. We worked for this very county until we couldn't take it any longer. We've had this store for the last fifteen years instead and have never been more satisfied." I heard her step back. "You can open your eyes again."

I blinked and immediately saw in my reflection that the smudge had been removed – along with what had to have been another shadow on the opposite eye, too. I looked to her in the mirror. "I really am *not* very good at that."

"It's not something you do," she nodded as she washed her hands in the small sink. "Which is why this room exists. We have clients – well, not really clients, but new friends perhaps – who are feeling their way forward as they explore their identities. Some are experimenting, others are embracing." She turned back toward me. "The important aspect is we don't judge any of them."

I glanced at Vasily, who picked up on my thoughts. Turning toward Anne, he asked: "You said 'teens such as Chase' a bit earlier. Can you tell us what you mean by that exactly?"

Anne continued to dry her hands with a small towel. "Normally, I would defer and deflect when someone asked me about a patron."

"Normally?" I echoed.

"Yeah," she nodded as she looped the towel over a hanger by the sink. "Given Chase is dead now, I'm even more reluctant to speak out of school."

I leaned around the chair and faced her. "I'll be candid, Anne. I think someone killed Chase; I don't know the *why* just yet, owing more to the fact that we're coming at this investigation backwards."

"Killed?" she asked, eyes wide. "Someone murdered him?"

"That's our operating assumption at this point," Vasily answered. "There are still a few moving pieces to our inquiries, but Sean is right. It wasn't an accident."

"Damn," she breathed as she sank down into a chair next to mine. "That changes things a bit."

"It does," I agreed.

Anne looked up at me. "Well, for starters, Chase was not here specifically for himself," she said. "He was pretty much what he seemed to be: a good kid with a definite sense of self." She smiled slightly. "And a penchant for coffee."

"I can relate to that part," I nodded. "You said he was a volunteer, though?"

"Yes, which is how I met him. He was also an incredibly supportive friend." She looked to Vasily. "A friend to someone who was struggling quite a bit with their own identity."

"In what way?"

"That's not entirely my story to tell," Anne replied softly. "Suffice it to say, Chase had an intimate connection with them, and had from the beginning."

"I need a name, Anne," I said equally as softly. "Can you provide one?"

She hesitated. "Let me call them and see if they will talk with you," she said after a long moment. "If the request comes from me, it might be more palatable. And less scary."

"I understand," I smiled. "And I appreciate whatever help you can provide."

"Wait here, if you don't mind?" she asked as she moved out of the room.

I watched her exit and turned to Vasily. "I am beginning to see a reason in the tea leaves," I said thoughtfully. "And I don't like the conclusion I'm coming to."

"Want to share your thoughts?" he said, arching an eyebrow.

"As soon as my latest hunch is confirmed," I smiled.

Vasily cocked his head at me and folded his arms. "I hate it when you do that," he said with a half-smile. "And like everything else, I've missed it."

"What?" I asked innocently.

"Solving the case."

I grinned slightly. "I wouldn't go that far," I replied. "Let's just say it's starting to come into focus."

He rolled his eyes but didn't have time to launch his witty retort before Anne appeared in the doorway. "I was able to speak to them," she said. "If you can hang out for a bit, they'll come over during their open period for a cup of coffee." She smiled slightly. "Rancho Linda High School has many problems, I assure you, but one of them is not the fact they have an open campus in this day and age. The kids truly learn how to manage their time when they know they can run about between classes."

Standing from the chair, I nodded. "I think we can do that," I smiled. "If you have WIFI, we might never leave."

"We do," she laughed.

"Then I'll get my laptop from the SUV while we wait for Bobbie."
Anne looked nonplussed. "How did you know it was Bobbie?"
Vasily started to laugh.

Twenty-Seven

Bobbie's open period started at ten according to a still flabbergasted Anne, so after running out to the SUV to pick up our materials, she set us up at a four–top over by the performance stage. At that early hour, not many folks were whiling away their time reading in the comfy loungers or doing the crossword over their coffee, so we had that part of the store to ourselves. It took very little time for us to spread files across the imitation cherry top.

"Coach Dalton thought Bobbie was his girlfriend," Vasily said once we had two steaming cups of the Mexican Organic and our laptops open. "Bobbie wasn't, was she?"

"You might have noticed that Anne went to great pains to use gender neutral pronouns when describing Bobbie," I pointed out. "I suspect Bobbie hasn't quite decided what they are, yet. We'll know more when they arrive."

Vasily nodded. "You're right. 'Bobbie' could go multiple ways, gender wise. Sorry."

"Add to that the fact the parents didn't mention Chase had a girl-friend, and I think we can conclude he probably didn't have one. Bobbie was a friend, of that I have no doubt; but as busy as Chase seems to have been, his efforts with them were more along the lines of moral support."

"I don't see how Bobbie figures into this now, then," Vasily said, tapping his cellphone against his chin. "Unless you think they were directly involved in the murder?"

"No, I don't think Bobbie was involved in the murder," I said. "As a cause, though, perhaps."

"I don't follow."

"You will," I smiled. "Make sure you record our interview with Bobbie on your phone, if you would."

An eyebrow was arched in my direction. "Don't trust my notetaking skills any longer? I'm hurt," he pouted dramatically.

"I want our bases to be covered, that's all," I replied.

He started to nod. "And you want a voice on tape. That we can check against the 9–1–1 call."

I tapped my nose with a finger. "Well done."

Vasily started to smile when his phone buzzed. "It's Parker Cromwell," he said as he stood and moved away from the table.

I nodded and turned back to my laptop. Admittedly, I was a bit late to the game in terms of reviewing Chase's social media, but I felt like I now had a pretty solid idea what I was going to find. It wasn't often that I had a lawyerly like moment, asking a question that I knew the answer to, but this appeared to be one of them. Chase appeared to like two of the three biggest platforms, with accounts on each. Neither was especially active, actually, leading me to think he was more of a consumer than a contributor. That wasn't terribly unusual, for I'd found over the years that only a tiny fraction of the public using social media were deeply engaged.

The rest of us just lurked.

Unsurprisingly, on both platforms he had liked or followed accounts related to tennis, UCLA, the *LA Times* and Cal Berkeley; there were also quite a number of social justice groups, including no fewer than fifteen in the LGBTQ space. *That* was remarkable for someone his age, though most college–aged students were trending toward being far more civil–rights oriented than even my own generation. Scanning the groups, all of them were thoughtful, mainstream organizations that supported the communities they served.

Sorting through more screens, I found he'd signed up for fundraisers and done five– and ten–kilometer races for charity; he'd RSVP'd for seminars on gender and identity issues, too. I was so engrossed in the depth of his passion for the space that I'd missed the fact Vasily had quietly reseated himself across from me more than thirty minutes earlier.

"Sean?" he asked quietly.

My eyes flicked up. "I take it all back. This kid was an extraordinary, one–of–a–kind specimen. The stuff he was following – the posts he was reading – speak to an emotional maturity far beyond his biological age."

"There can occasionally be gems in the wild," he smiled. "Parker apologized. Their first grandchild was born yesterday, and he and Adele went up the coast to be with their daughter. He said he'd come back if we needed him."

"Odd that he didn't mention his daughter was pregnant."

"You of all people know that interviewees tend not to tell us more than we ask."

"Indeed," I nodded. "We still need to talk to him, but it can wait. We'll FaceTime if we have to."

"That's what I told him. Did you take a look at the photos that were deleted yet?" he asked.

"My next stop," I said as I pulled up the archive I'd dropped onto my laptop. "What are you in to?"

"I've got those full cell records to peruse," he said. "And I've just gotten the forensics back on the van. Let me scan that first."

"Sounds good."

Faced with hundreds of megabytes of images, I resorted everything by date and started with the earliest I could find. Though I'd not investigated many cases involving a person in Chase's age range, I was unsurprised with the sheer number of selfies, taken in all sorts of locations. There were also a ton of candid photos of friends and family doing normal–seeming activities, and quite a few of the very space we were in, though with a band playing and appreciative patrons clapping.

Ordinary. Normal. Nothing seemed out of place.

Except...

I scrolled backwards and found the shot that had triggered something. It was a selfie, and it looked like Chase was behind the wheel of the minivan. He was wearing a white head kerchief with the logo of the school, tying back his wild mane of blond hair, and had leaned his head against a striking young woman. For her part, she, too, appeared to be wearing a similar head wrap, tying back her long, black hair; only a tiny part of her t–shirt was visible, but it seemed to be the same as what Chase was wearing,

Keeping that file open, I searched through others and couldn't find another shot of him dressed that way. Heart pounding slightly, I clicked into the metadata of the photo in question and determined it had been taken no more than two hours before the first 9–1–1 call had been made.

"Shit," I said.

Vasily looked up, startled. "What?"

"This was the final picture Chase took," I said as I turned my MacBook toward him.

His eyes widened. "Bobbie?" he said, looking up.

"Yes," came a deep voice from our side. "That's me."

We both turned to see a version of the photo standing beside us, though it wasn't quite the same. Bobbie was presenting as male this time out, with the long black hair tied up in a masculine ponytail not dissimilar to Vasily's, and attired in the standard unisex warmups all athletes received. Without makeup, a slight shading of stubble was evident along the soft cheekbones; while it was clear the eyebrows had been professionally shaped, the eyelashes were far shorter without the extensions. Faux diamond studs in each ear replaced the hoops from the photo.

I stood up and held out my hand. "I'm Chief Colbeth," I greeted, feeling the firm grasp as we shook. "Call me Sean, please. And this is my colleague, Detective Korsokovach."

"Vasily," he said with a smile as he shook.

"Thanks for taking time to join us," I said as I waved to an empty chair. "I assume this is a tough subject for you."

"It is."

"Before we go too far, I want to make sure we address you properly," I started. "You go by Bobbie?"

"I do." There was a pause. "Bobbie McCallen."

"And... if you don't mind my asking, how are you identifying today?"

That brought a smile. "So few people take the time to ask that. Right now? Male, I guess," he said before his eyes flicked to my screen. "Though it was female when we took that photo."

"You're not on the tennis team, are you?"

"No. Track and Field."

I nodded and turned back to the photo. "This seems like it was quite the occasion."

Bobbie smiled a bit more. "That was the culmination of months of hard work," he said, his eyes glistening slightly.

"Look," I said quietly, "if you don't want to talk about this, we can schedule another time. I understand completely—"

"No," Bobbie said firmly. "I'm here because I want to be. *Need* to be."

"Okay." I tapped the screen. "Tell me about this."

"It was my first day – or was going to be my first full day – expressing as female," he said softly. "It's taken me years to get to a point where I will even allow myself the freedom to *consider* I am the wrong gender, biologically," he added as he looked up. "Chase is – *was* – one of my closest friends and has been for years. He knew I was struggling and hooked me up with one of the foundations that meets in this space a few times a month."

"He sounds like a rare find," I said, looking to Vasily.

"Chase was amazing. No matter how crazy his schedule was, he always managed to be there for me – especially when I started my first tentative steps toward that day."

"Walk me through it."

Bobbie reached out and touched Chase's face with a carefully manicured fingertip. "Both of us had optional Saturday practice," Bobbie began. "Not one to usually lie, Chase told his parents he'd be at school and I did the same. Instead, Chase met me here." Bobbie looked up. "That photo was taken after Anne and Chase watched me finally do my hair and makeup on my own. The plan then was drive down to Anaheim and go to Disneyland for the day."

He looked away. "Chase had scrounged up the cash for two tickets. He thought I'd feel more comfortable transitioning among the weekend crowds at the park." Bobbie looked up. "I'd be hiding in plain sight, and he was willing to be there just to make sure I was comfortable."

"Obviously you didn't get there," Vasily said softly. "What happened?"

Bobbie dropped his hand back to the surface of the table. "We made good time and got to Disneyland, then parked the car in that massive garage they have." He looked at me, and I could see the sadness in his eyes. "It was too much, though. As I was riding the escalator down to where the trams take you to the park, I panicked. Chase kept reassuring me it would be fine, that we could get through it together; it didn't work. I froze at the security checkpoint, and I mean *froze* completely. I don't remember how we got back to the minivan, but the next thing I *do* recall is Chase turning back onto Interstate Five to get back here."

"He brought you back to the shop?"

"Yes," Bobbie said. "My car was in the lot, for starters; and I knew Anne would help me shed the makeup. The hoops were hers, too, so I wanted to return them." Bobbie looked back at the photo. "He was so... Chase. He knew I was in a bad way, so he took me around to the rear entrance. Anne and Zoe let some of the regulars use it if we want to avoid seeing people in the mall."

I kept my face impassive. "Where did he park, exactly?"

Bobbie looked at me. "I'm not sure, to be honest. Close to the door? I think there was a big dumpster close by."

I nodded. "And he came in with you?"

"Yes." He looked back at Chase on my laptop. "Got me straight to Anne; I was a total wreck at that point. It took the rest of the morning to calm down. I'd let everyone down, including myself."

"I'm sure that's not the case," I said. "Just the fact you even drove down to Anaheim means a lot."

Bobbie turned to me. "Funny. That's the last thing Chase said to me, before he left to move his van."

"I'm not surprised, from what I know of him." I paused again. "When was that?"

"I have no idea," Bobbie replied. "I mean, given how traffic was that day, and how long the round–trip might have been, maybe ninety minutes from when that photo was taken."

"Were you surprised when Chase didn't reappear?" Vasily asked.

"I was a mess, Detective," Bobbie replied. "I didn't realize entirely where *I* was until Anne brought me a slice of pizza from the food court. When it dawned on me, I snarfed down the food and returned home, tail between my legs."

"Were you in love with Chase?" I asked.

Bobbie smiled. "Now that is a hard question to answer," he said. "Maybe? Some part of me? But I knew it would never bear fruit, so I was content to have him as my friend." He shook his head a bit. "To be honest, until I figure out who I am, exactly, it's not fair for me to get involved with anyone romantically."

I nodded. "That is very honorable."

"Yeah," Bobbie said as he pushed up to leave. "Doesn't make the loneliness hurt any less, I assure you."

Twenty-Eight

Owing to the hour – and another promise to be available for the afternoon of panels at the convention – we packed up and drove back to the hotel in Anaheim and had lunch with Suzanne once more, though for a change of pace, we regrouped at the all–day restaurant across the way at the Hilton. Suzanne had beaten us to the punch and was already in costume for the afternoon, though I didn't recognize the outfit. Instead of the usual red spandex with black polka dots, she was dressed in unrelieved black with neon green accents, a black mask and had a wig of long black hair in a braid. By the time I got to the two triangular ears atop the wig, I thought I had a bit of a clue.

"That's my character, but not," I said with a bemused expression as we sat down. I'd long stopped noticing the panoply of characters we now dined with on a regular basis. To be honest, aside from the waitstaff, Vasily and I were the only two *not* dressed up.

"Do you like it?" Suze asked. "I found it on the vendor floor this morning. I couldn't believe they had our size! This is from an episode where the two main characters exchange their jewels. Ladybug becomes Lady Noire, and Chat becomes Mister Bug."

"That's clever," I said before realizing Vasily was dying. "What?"

"I cannot *wait* to see you with earrings," he said.

I looked between the two of them. "Hang on. Did you say 'our size?'"

"I did."

"Now wait just a damn minute–––"

"You needed a change of pace," Suzanne said sweetly.

"Not one that comes with piercings."

"They're clip on. Humor me."

I looked at the cute smile she offered and melted. "My God," I said as I sagged into my seat. "What have I gotten into this time?"

"A very tight red–and–black number," Vasily chortled. "Oh, this is gonna be good."

I glared at him.

"Don't worry, I'll be right there with you," he said. "I brought my Black Spider–Man suit for tonight. And I need to get your photo on social media afterwards."

I rolled my eyes.

"Speaking of," Suzanne interjected. "How's the case going?"

"Well," I said as our drink order arrived. "We've more or less definitively located where Chase died; we think we've spoken with the second–to–last person to see him alive, too."

"You're not going to work tomorrow, are you?" she asked. "It's the second to the last day of the convention! Most of the big panels and big stars will be here."

"Maybe just the morning?" I said, shooting a glance to Vasily. "It depends on how quickly we get through what we need to review this afternoon."

"Can I help?" she asked sincerely. "I can look through anything you need me to."

"I might have you glance at the coroner's report later, if you don't mind."

"Happy to do it," she said. "Oh! I nearly forgot. The front desk manager called the room and left a message; he needs to talk to you straight away."

"How urgent was it?" I asked, raising my eyebrows.

"I'm not sure, to be honest."

I pushed back from the table. "Go ahead and order," I said as I stood. "Let me see what's up."

"Do you want me to get something started for you?" Suzanne asked.

"No, I'll be right back. But don't wait."

I hurried out of the restaurant and through the double glass doors of the lobby, unusually unsettled by the summons from the hotel. Dashing across the parkway between the hotels, I presented myself to the registration desk and in short order was facing a tall man with a friendly smile.

"Chief Colbeth," he said pleasantly. "Harold Kincaid. My apologies, but I must ask if you have another form of payment for your room. The card we have on file is being declined."

I raised my eyebrows. "That's unusual," I said. "It's actually our purchasing card from the town."

"I know," Harold said with a smile. "And yet, we are not able to use it."

Pulling out my wallet, I retrieved my personal credit card and handed it to him. "Here," I said. "This one should be good."

"Give me just a moment to update your portfolio," he said as he whisked away with my card.

While I waited, I unlocked my iPhone and dialed Caitlyn back in Windeport. She picked up on the first ring. "Chief," she said. "What's going on?" she asked, a bit urgently. "They've been changing the locks in the building all day today. I didn't realize you'd asked for that."

"I didn't," I said, my heart sinking. "And my P–card was declined here at the hotel."

There was a long pause. "Shit."

"Yeah."

"Hang on. Let me call Sal over at the Council office."

"Okay."

Caitlyn put me on hold and I listened to the static for a few moments before she came back on the line. "Those *bastards*," she said loud enough I had to hold my phone out from my ear.

"They voted me out, didn't they?"

"Yes! Retroactive to *Monday*," she cried before lowering her voice. "We didn't actually think they'd go with the lawyer's recommendation. Bastards."

I nodded. "They have a village to run. And want a fresh start."

"No," Caitlyn fumed. "They have to be blind to overlook what you've done for this place."

"Caitlyn, don't worry about it."

"But they cancelled everything! You'll have to pay out of pocket now!"

"Do I still have the plane ticket?"

"Let me check." I heard her typing on the computer. "Yeah, apparently it was too much trouble to cancel since they wouldn't get any money back."

I smiled. It wasn't much, but... "Cancel it."

"Are you sure? You'll be stranded out there."

"I'll get home, don't worry," I said. "And since it looks like I'm going to be in California for a few more days anyway, can you make sure my office gets packed up properly?"

"I will," she said. "Where do you want your stuff to go?"

"Drop it in Suzanne's office. Someone is covering for her while we're here."

"Got it," she said. "Damn, Chief. This is so many levels of wrong."

"I know," I said. "But maybe it was time for me to part ways with the Village anyway."

"Call me if you need anything," she said. "I mean that."

"I know you do. Thanks," I said as I hung up.

Harold re–appeared with a smile. "Thank you, sir. I'm sorry for the trouble."

"So am I," I smiled back.

As I walked back toward the Hilton, I called Mike. "Hey Sean," he said, "I was wondering when I'd hear from you."

"I've got a lot to talk about," I confirmed. "But first, can we make a tiny change in our agreement...?"

Twenty-Nine

Owing to my new circumstances, I opted for a liquid lunch and was on my third gin and tonic when Suzanne had finally calmed down to the point of no longer threatening to take out everyone on the Village Council with strategically thrown scalpels. "I knew it was coming," I sighed. "I just assumed they wouldn't be so chickenshit about it."

"But your *career*! This *case*!"

"Oh, I'm still getting paid for my work," I smiled. "I've already spoken to Mike. He was more than happy to adjust the contract and make me an 'outside consultant' – which actually comes with a raise."

"Regardless," Vasily said, arms folded. "Come stay with me. Save some cash and check out tomorrow."

"That's a nice offer," I said, "but I don't want to impose."

"Nonsense," he replied. "It's just for a few more days anyway, right?"

"I've got to leave on Sunday," Suzanne said. "I need to be back at my practice."

"I think we'll have everything wrapped soon," I smiled. "Your ticket is still good, since I paid for that out of pocket. Mine is the only one that needs to be rebooked."

Suzanne looked at me. "You're still coming home, right? After this is over?"

"Yes," I said.

"Good, because without you there to stop me, there's no telling whether I'll implement my evil plan to eliminate the Village Council."

"Have no fear, Milady," I said, and winked. "To be honest, this is a bit of a load off of me. I might actually enjoy wearing that outfit of yours."

We all stood to leave, and she leaned over to kiss me. "And I will enjoy seeing you wear it."

"I'm sure," I replied with a smile.

Parting ways with Suzanne at the parkway, I looked at Vasily. "You really were the smart one, you know that, right?"

"I'm not sure about that," he said as we started to randomly walk along the promenade. "I can't say my experience here has been any better than what you are going through – went through."

We came to the edge of a small fountain and I sat against the concrete, with Vasily joining to one side. "I've thought about striking out on my own a few times. I've even considered taking that position with the State Police Captain Roberts keeps tossing at me. More so after you left," I added as I leaned back on my arms. "The joy of the job vanished when you took off," I said. "We did do good work together. For years."

"We did. And we still do," he said softly.

I looked at him. "Yeah. We do." I smiled a bit crookedly. "What are your thoughts about going private?"

"Are you asking what I think you're asking?"

"Maybe," I nodded. "I might have lost my job, but I still have national connections. It would mean travel, until we decide where we want to land for good. I'd have to stay in Windeport for a bit, since Suzanne just took over the practice. But it's dying on her – literally. The population is declining faster than any of us realized."

"How long?"

"Four years, maybe five before she has to combine with another physician just to break even."

Vasily looked at me with a crooked smile. "I am having a hard time believing you would leave Windeport. I think your lunch is speaking."

"It's just loosened up some thoughts that have been rattling around since November," I said honestly. "Frankly, my father might have had the right idea. Get away to some place with better weather. And better beaches."

"That doesn't leave too many places to consider," Vas smiled. "But to answer your question, yes, I would join you if you struck out and went private. I'm not up on what it takes to go that route, though."

"I know a guy," I smiled. "Let me run some numbers and we'll talk after this mess is over."

"Okay," he replied. "Now, seeing as though you are in a weakened state emotionally, maybe you'll tell me who you think killed Chase?"

I sighed. "It's only a hunch, Vas. And I have no evidence to back it up. Yet."

Watching some birds fly over the park area in formation, I crossed my arms as I straightened up against the cold concrete. I had to remind myself that it was subzero back in Maine; here I was in a polo and khakis, enjoying a nice sunny day. *I could get used to this*, I thought.

"I'm sure whatever happened went down shortly after Chase left Bobbie at *The Alternative Way*, and I'm quite certain now it was over a mistaken idea of *why* he was there." I looked back at Vasily. "But where I go off the rails is when I try to reconcile the term paper mill he had going on the side; it's clear now that was where he got the cash to treat Bobbie to a day at Disneyland. I looked up the prices – it's not cheap!"

"How does that create a problem?"

"It's an anomaly. Did he have competition in that space? Was someone upset at his work, or got caught? As unlikely as it sounds, it's plausible the location was just simply the opportunity the killer needed and has no special significance."

"But he *was* moved."

"Yes," I replied. "And that is why I think my first theory fits. *Where* Chase was found was significant to the killer, but maybe for the wrong reason. On another level, I could make the same judgement about whoever moved him, too." I paused. "If they aren't the same person."

"That would make his father a suspect!"

"Maybe. We didn't get a chance to ask him *where* he found the minivan yet. But it is also probable – and still quite likely – he found Chase four hours later and moved the van to preserve what he thought was a secret that needed protecting."

Vasily blinked. "I feel like I am missing something, for you seem short of suspects again."

I smiled slightly. "Not really. There are at least two people left in the field that would have a lot to lose if they presumed Chase wasn't who he purported to be, and therefore unable to do what he was supposed to do."

"What the hell are you saying?"

"Let me put it another way. What if you were, say, the person trusted to connect students with colleges – and after placing one, you get wind that they are thinking of, shall we say, changing teams?"

Vasily's eyes widened. "The guidance counselor? I can't see that."

"Me either, but it's a possible motive. Tenuous."

"At best."

"Or, maybe you are –"

"Shit," Vasily said. "Coach Dalton."

"Exactly. He's watched Chase move up through the ranks, and after all the years of work as his coach – personal and scholastically – he finally has that top–tier recruit. *Male* recruit. Then, somehow – and this is the part we need to nail down – he thinks he discovers Chase is gender fluid. And that his star pupil is about to shit on his parade. Big time."

"We have part of it, don't we? He knew about Bobbie. Called him Chase's girlfriend."

I nodded. "A slip. The first one." I sighed. "We need to place him at the mall close to when we think Chase made the call. And I need his voice on tape."

Vasily shook his head. "That part doesn't fit, Sean. If he were apoplectic about Chase possibly changing gender, the last thing he'd want is to have Chase discovered at *The Alternative Way*."

"Yeah," I nodded. "You're right. I *can* see him panicking and leaving Chase behind, but I am still stumped at how Chase wound up under that seat. The one thing I am certain of, though, is Chase *didn't* make the call. Either of them. I'll need Suzanne to review the coroner's report to confirm that part for me, though."

Vasily slowly nodded. "We're going to optional tennis practice to-morrow, aren't we?"

"Just as soon as Suzanne and I move our gear over to your place in the morning," I smiled.

Thirty

I knew I was riding alcohol–fueled high emotions when I found I'd been staring out the window of our soon–to–be–former hotel room for nearly an hour. Instead of reviewing the files one more time with Vasily, who had joined me in the room to do just that, I'd instead observed the increasing crowd as the convention kicked into high gear. Somewhere in all of the information we'd collected, there was a thread that connected Dalton Ramsfeld to our murder; a few hours of attention would likely find it, but I seemed to not have any desire to dig in like I normally would.

Looking at the clock radio by the bed, I turned a sheepish smile on my friend. "I'm sorry," I said as I wandered back toward the small table cluttered with files and two sleek laptops. "My heart isn't in this at the moment. Even though I know we are very close."

Vasily looked up, sliding a loose bang back behind an ear. "Who could blame you?" he smiled. "It's not like you just got fired from your full–time gig, or anything."

I slumped into the chair opposite. "I think I need a break," I said as I looked longingly back at the window. "I can't believe I'm saying this, but I think I'm falling in love with the weather here."

"We do that to people," he laughed. "A few more days and California will own your soul."

"Shit," I chuckled. "I'd better escape." I ran a hand through my curls and had a thought. "How far away is that garage Bobbie told us about?"

"The one that Chase parked in?" he asked. "Maybe two miles from here. It's on the far side of the park."

I looked at him, a slight smile on my face. "Wanna go for a run?"

Vasily arched an eyebrow, his eyes bright with inquiry. "What on earth do you think you'll find if we hike out there?"

"I don't know, honestly," I replied. "Sometimes seeing places even tangentially connected to the crime flesh out the narrative." I shrugged. "And I just don't have it in me to trudge through spreadsheets and databases this afternoon."

He laughed. "All right. Lucky for you, my gear's in the SUV," he said. "Let me grab it and we'll go."

Less than twenty minutes later, we were once more outfitted in our appropriate running attire, trotting through the crowd in front of the Anaheim Convention Center. Vasily was more familiar with the area than I was, though I quickly recognized we were at least starting off in the same direction as the evening I'd walked up to have dinner with Suzanne. However, instead of tacking right once we hit one of the two Disney hotels on Magic Way, he continued beneath an overpass and came up on the other side in front of a massive multi-level parking structure.

Crossing with the light, Vasily found a pathway into a hedge that gave access to the security checkpoint and tram loading area Bobbie had mentioned. The garage was on two sides of the space, with escalators of varying heights quietly humming away connecting the upper reaches to ground level. Despite the late hour, business appeared to be brisk with multiple airport-style security checkpoint lines moving people through metal detectors. Just beyond was a similarly smooth operation loading people onto ten- or fifteen-car long trams.

"The metal detectors started a few years ago," Vasily said as we paused the workout on our respective watches. "It's a bit sad to go through them on your way to the Happiest Place on Earth."

Stretching a quad out behind me, I nodded in agreement. "A particular commentary on our times." Shielding my eyes against the late afternoon sunshine, I tried to wrap my brain around how big the garage was. "This is huge," I finally observed.

"The original – the one to your right – held ten thousand cars. I think the newer section has at least that many as well."

"I wouldn't want to be here when both of these are full."

"No," he laughed. "You wouldn't." He pointed to the escalator coming down from the right portion. "Based on when he said they got here, I'd assume Chase parked in that structure since it's usually the first one filled. We could confirm that with Disney."

I blinked. "Do they have cameras in this thing?" I asked.

"Yeah," Vasily said. "Why?"

"Please tell me you are hiding your badge somewhere in all of that Spandex, because I don't have mine."

Vasily rolled his eyes. "Oh sure. I *totally* have a hidden compartment you *can't see* in these skintight leggings."

"Don't worry," I said. "I have an idea. Downtown Disney is back that way?"

"Yeah," he said, frowning. "Why?"

"Follow me," I laughed as I started back up my workout and jogged away from him backwards. "And all will be revealed."

"God, I hope so," Vasily lamented.

I retraced our steps and sent up a silent prayer as we approached the original checkpoint I'd gone through a few days earlier. Scanning the various security lines, I felt my smile widen as I located the memorable figure of the Disney Security officer I'd run into.

Trotting over to where he was chatting with a few colleagues, he caught my approach and broke off his conversation. "Is it casual day at the office?" he laughed as he held out his hand.

"Forced PT," I chuckled as I shook his hand. "Bob, this is my colleague and friend, Vasily Korsokovach." I laughed a bit more. "My name is Sean Colbeth. I neglected that part during our earlier conversation."

"Nice to meet you," Bob said. "Here to take me up on the offer?"

"Offer?" Vasily asked, frowning deeper as he turned to me.

"I'm more open to it than I was earlier," I laughed. "But actually, I was wondering if you could help us out a bit."

"Sure," he said with a smile. "What do you need?"

"We're investigating a case for the Rancho Linda department—"

"Mike Gilbert's turf?" he chuckled. "How's the old grizzly doing?"

"Fine," I replied with a half–smile. "You know Mike?"

"Sure. His kids swim with my grandkids. I see him at meets all the time; I pegged him for a cop the moment he walked on deck." He looked at me anew. "What work are you doing?"

"I'm out from my own department in Maine," I explained, "helping Vasily get some background on a high school student who died a while back."

Bob's eyes widened. "You mean that kid in the back of the minivan?" he asked. "I thought it was an accident."

"Well, you know how it goes," Vasily replied. "Once you start pulling a thread…"

"I do," he replied. "Thirty years as a detective in Seattle taught me that."

"We have a lead that the morning of the accident, the kid in question came here to the park; we believe he used the parking structure back there," I added, pointed in the general direction of the massive concrete edifice. "I'd like to confirm that if I can, and wondered who I'd talk to about possibly reviewing the video of the ticket booth or the garage it-self."

Bob frowned. "The Company has a pretty strict policy with respect to co–operating with authorities," he said slowly. "Which is a poor way of saying, unless you get the department's lawyers to reach out, you're not likely to get anything out of us."

"Ah," I said, feeling a bit crestfallen. "Totally understandable."

"I'm truly sorry I couldn't have been more help," he said.

"No worries," I replied. "It was good to see you again, though."

"Same," Bob smiled. "Say," he added after a moment, "before you go, have you ever seen our operations center?"

I blinked. "No," I said.

"Come on," he said as he put an arm around me. "Let me give you a tour."

"Uh... okay..." I stammered. "I'm not exactly in professional dress, Bob," I protested as he propelled me through the magnetron, with Vasily close behind.

Bob chuckled. "You wouldn't be the first Lycra–cladded person roaming Backstage. It is Disney, after all. Come on, this way," he said as he redirected us toward a side entrance that was cleverly camouflaged behind some bushes.

A few steps away from the fantastical surroundings of the exterior found us in a very ordinary looking industrial alleyway, with small portable office buildings here and there, as well as what appeared to be rear entrances into shops or restaurants facing the customers. "This is... not what I expected," I said honestly.

Bob laughed again. "We only theme what Guests see," he explained.

"Guests?"

"That's what we call people who come to the park," he explained. "Onstage – where the show is – those folks are considered our Guests. Backstage is where all of the operational magic happens."

"Clever," I said.

We weaved our way around employees ("Cast Members," Bob corrected me) hustling to keep the "show" humming; I was a bit floored at how many people were scurrying here and there, knowing there were at least as many "on stage," too. "This is pretty busy," I observed.

"The parade starts in twenty minutes," Bob explained. "It's usually pandemonium ensuring it starts on time. Which it does, each and every day."

"That is astounding," I said, totally floored. "I had no idea what went on here. I thought it was just rollercoasters."

"Well, we have those for sure," Bob laughed. "But we specialize in the experience." He paused at the bottom of a short staircase. "You've never been to the park, have you?"

"No," I replied. "I mean, years ago I was here with my girlfriend at the time. But we never made it inside."

"We'll have to fix that," he laughed. "Come on, Security is this way."

In short order, we were in a medium-sized room set up Mission Control style, with a massive wall of projected images across the front, and three rows of consoles on successively higher tiers facing them. Bob moved over to an unused console in the rear and pulled up an extra chair. "We have three of these centers on site," he explained. "This one covers Disneyland, and has a sister station over at the other park. The third is in Team Disney and acts as backup."

"Team Disney?"

He laughed and lowered his voice. "It's what they call the building out back where the bean counters work. No one wants to get posted there."

"You have some strange naming schemes in this company."

"Don't I know it." He punched in an access code on the console and twin monitors lit up. "When did your kid arrive?" he asked.

Vasily gave him the date. "We think it was fairly early – close to eight maybe?"

Bob punched in something. "Lucky for you, I am a senior supervisor," he said quietly. "That means I can do this kind of search without attracting attention."

"I appreciate this, Bob."

"My pleasure." He hit an execute key and a few moments later, the screen lit up with small thumbnails of video, each with a five-minute index. "What are we looking for?"

"Late model minivan, brown, two teenagers." I looked at Vasily. "A... couple."

Bob punched in something and the thumbnails shifted. "Here," he said as he tapped an image with a finger, enlarging it.

I whistled. "How did you do that?" I asked. It was a clear shot of Chase and Bobbie, taken from the passenger side of the van. Bobbie had her hair pulled back into twin ponytails, and though she was smiling, looked a little nervous.

"Artificial Intelligence has changed our security around here," he said. "I'm not a huge fan of it – shades of Terminator for me – but it has it's uses."

"That's them," I said. "Can you track them?"

"Give me a few minutes," he said.

Bob punched a few keys and the shot returned to the original wide angle, one that captured the unique double-sided ticket booth arrangement in the parking garage. Vehicles pulled up along a two-lane strip of asphalt and were easily served either from the driver's side or, as was the case with Chase, the passenger's side. As Bob allowed the image to roll forward, I was enthralled for a moment by the efficiency of the operation, for it allowed Disney to handle two cars at once; it was as elegant as clockwork, for as soon as two cars pulled away, two more replaced them. I'm not sure why, but a waltz I'd heard as a kid by Johann Strauss suddenly popped into my head, perfectly timed to the movements of the vehicles. I was about to comment on my musical metaphor when something about the next set of vehicles caught my eye.

"Hang on," I said suddenly. "Can you get me a clearer shot of *that* vehicle?" I asked Bob, pointing to a sedan that had pulled up to the booth working the driver's side.

"Sure," Bob said as he sorted the shots. A moment later, it exploded full screen on a third monitor; the memorably unique shape of the parking sticker from Rancho Linda High School alone would have attracted my attention, if not the face of the driver that was now in full view. "This one?" he asked.

"Yeah," I said, looking to Vasily.

"Holy *Hell*," Vasily breathed.

I looked back at the image of Dalton Ramsfeld, in the same lane but two cars behind Chase and Bobbie. "You could say that again."

"I take it that's a person of interest?" Bob asked with a slight smile.

"Yes," I replied without hesitation. "Can you tag that vehicle, too?"

"Sure," he said as he tapped a few more commands into his console.

We spent the better part of an hour with Bob, reviewing the footage from the parking garage. Beyond the initial shot of Chase paying at the attendant, he managed to find video of the minivan pulling into a spot on the floor marked as *Daisy* as well as footage of it backing out of the space less than ten minutes later (according to the timestamp). That much supported Bobbie's story about their aborted trip to the park.

"There are multiple cameras on the escalators," Bob said as he queued up something in the ballpark of time after the minivan parked. We managed to catch Chase and Bobbie among the crowd headed down, Chase talking and Bobbie apparently just listening. Finding them returning was even easier, since the preeminent flow was *down*; they were the only pair headed *up* during the same window of time.

What caused my eyebrows to go up was the fact they were both taking the steps two at a time, clearly in a hurry to get back to the minivan. Bobbie even tossed a look over her shoulder more than once.

"So far, it fits what she told us," I said, looking at Vasily before tapping a finger on the frozen image. "That, though, concerns me."

"People don't usually run *away* from the park," Bob observed dryly.

"Is there anything at the bottom of the escalator? Something must have happened before they attempted to board the trams."

"I should," he said as he tapped a bit on the keypad and opened a new window. "This is on top of the hedge looking toward the security area," Bob explained. "And about when they came down the escalator."

He ran the video forward and we caught the duo as they stepped off the escalator and started toward the security checkpoint. Bobbie and Chase moved to get into a line when a figure came up to Chase and whirled him around.

"Freeze that," I asked, and Bob touched something, pausing on a shot of the third figure as they held an angry finger up and in Chase's face. "Is that Dalton?"

Vasily leaned in, and I caught a whiff of his cologne mixed with anti–perspirant; they were oddly compatible fragrances. "Maybe?" he said, squinting. "The shot is too far out to tell for sure."

"There might be another angle," Bob said. "Give me a moment."

I looked at Vasily again. "Who matches their cologne and anti–perspirant?" I whispered.

"Who *wouldn't?*" he smiled. "This puts Dalton in contact with Chase within the hour."

"I know," I said. "If it's him."

"Got it," Bob said and maxed another window. It was a tighter shot from a different angle, and clearly caught Dalton from the front. "That your guy?"

"It is," I murmured. "Can you play the rest?"

"Yep."

We watched as Dalton appeared to say something heated to Chase, who stepped in front of Bobbie before calmly replying. That seemed to incense Dalton further; Chase continued to calmly stand there, but Bobbie started to shake her head before breaking for the escalator. Chase remained long enough to say a final word or two to Dalton before taking off after Bobbie.

"And he stays...?" I asked, watching as Dalton stood there in the security area. "Why?"

"He still looks angry," Vasily observed. "But must have gotten whatever it was off of his chest? Maybe?"

"Maybe," I replied.

We watched a few more moments before Dalton started to walk toward the escalators himself.

"And there we have it," Vasily sighed. "That will be damning in court."

"If you ever get this footage from us," Bob reminded us. "Which I suspect you won't, since Disney would work very hard to ensure it's not connected to a crime of any kind."

"Understood," I replied. "I think we have enough, anyway. But just to complete my own mental image, can you trace the car Dalton was in?"

Bob smiled. "I figured you'd ask for that; give me a second to pull the tag I added to it."

"Thank you for doing this, Bob," I said. "You truly don't know how much help this has been."

"I do, actually," he smiled as he worked his magic on the console. "I had someone do this same sort of favor for me many years ago in Seattle. Broke open a case that had haunted me for months." He tapped another sequence and a new video popped up. "Here we are, tight on the car from start to finish."

We watched as the video rolled from Dalton paying his own parking fee, to parking a few cars down from Chase in the same row, to pulling back out again about three minutes after Chase departed. "I don't have anything on the exit, I'm afraid," Bob apologized. "Once they are off property, it's Anaheim's turf. You'd have to talk to them to see what they might have for traffic video."

"We'll speak with them if it gets that far," I replied. "I think just the *hint* that we know all of this, though, and might be able to back it up in court may well get us what we need."

"Cool," Bob said as he shut down everything and stood. "Now, how would you like to ride Space Mountain?"

Thirty-One

Bob snuck us through the back door of several of the most popular attractions at Disneyland, treating us for all the world as though we were two high profile VIPs; I was surprised once more that no one gave a second thought to our unusual park–going attire but set it aside to accommodate my newfound admiration at what an interesting place Disneyland actually was. By the time I'd reluctantly told Bob we needed to get back to the hotel, I found myself understanding why Suzanne was so enraptured with the place.

"Thank you for everything," I said again as he walked us up to the turnstiles below the train station that fronted the park. "A tour with all the trimmings was an unexpected bonus."

"My pleasure," he smiled. "And it's part of my long–term strategy to get you to consider joining us when you retire."

"I will give it serious consideration."

"Good," he laughed as we pushed our way through the turnstiles and out into the massive esplanade.

"We'll have to hoof it to make it back before Suzanne gets annoyed," Vasily warned me as we broke into a jog. "We have less than an hour before we need to be in the grand ballroom."

"Shit," I breathed. "And I have to try and get into that new costume she bought me."

Traffic worked against us, but somehow, we managed to race all the way back to the hotel at a far faster pace than our run out to the garage;

fortunately, we found the hotel room empty when we arrived which gave me a moment to lean against the side wall to catch my breath. Hands on hips, my eyes caught the red–and–black polka dotted outfit carefully laid out across our king bed and felt my eyes roll.

"Dear Lord," I sighed. "That looks smaller than my other costume. I'm just gonna wear—"

"No, we stick to the plan," Vasily interrupted. "And it will stretch."

I reached over and felt the fabric. "It won't leave much to the imagination," I lamented.

"Nor should it," he chuckled.

"You are *no* help at all," I groaned as I snatched the costume and wig from the bed and headed for the bathroom. "If I'm not back in ten minutes—"

"You're on your own," Vasily laughed as he unzipped the duffel he'd brought up earlier, pulling a shimmery black outfit out. "I have my own issues to deal with."

A quarter of an hour later, I emerged from the bathroom, freshly showered and attired in my new threads. As I had feared, it was quite small and very uncomfortable in particular areas; I found myself unable to keep from pulling at the fabric in certain places to try and get relief from the pressure, and I was surprised at suddenly missing the hand-made quality of the costume Charlie had created for me.

The blond wig was similar to the Chat Noir one, sans ears, and Suzanne had carefully placed the mask and adhesive in the bathroom, leaving nothing to chance. Spinning in the closet mirror just outside the bathroom, I had to admit the overall effect was pretty stunning, right down to the matching red and black polka–dotted boots. Still, I'd gotten used to my *other* costume and felt myself unconsciously looking for the belt tail and ears.

"Not bad," Vasily said from beside me.

"I don't know," I said as I turned and stopped, mid–thought. For Vasily was standing in front of the windows covered head–to–toe in black spandex, a stylized white spider on his chest. His face had two white eye panels, and as he turned, I could see a similar spider design on his back. "Wow," I breathed.

"That's the best you've got?" he laughed. "I'll have you know this was the better part of a month's pay."

"Wow," was all I could say again as I nodded. "I have to hand it to you, I'm not sure I have the self–confidence to go out in public dressed like that."

Vasily laughed again. "Says the guy in a similarly form–fitting out-fit," he observed.

"Point taken," I smiled. "But I will be hiding behind my date all night."

"Scaredy cat," he teased.

"That's scaredy–bug to you, mister."

Suzanne chose that moment to return from the convention and found the two of us standing by the mirrored closet as she came through the door. "Up to no good, I see," she smiled as she leaned over to kiss me on the cheek.

"We'll never tell," Vasily said as he pulled the face mask off.

"Thick as thieves, indeed," she laughed as she stepped back to take a better look at me. "That fits... snugger than I thought it would."

"At the risk of getting in trouble... I miss my Chat costume."

Spinning me around, she nodded. "Yeah," she said. "This isn't you. Go ahead and change."

"Are you sure?" I asked. "I don't want to disappoint you."

"You couldn't do that," she said, kissing me again. "Go change so we can get a bite of dinner before the next panel."

Sliding the wig off, I started back toward the bathroom before paus-ing. "Actually – would you mind taking a peek at the coroner's report for me?"

"Sure," she said.

"I can bring it up on my laptop for her," Vasily said. "I think the forensic report arrived this afternoon, too."

"Anything of interest?" I asked as I snagged the Chat costume out of the closet and started to carefully peel the mask off. "Like, say, unknown fingerprints?"

"Let me look," he said.

Shucking back out of the costume was harder than getting it on, but at length I found myself staring at a more normal costumed figure in the mirror. I had to admit, I was getting pretty good at putting on the eye black and gluing the mask back on; a few more days of this and I'd be able to do it in the dark with my eyes closed.

Wrapping my belt tail around my waist as I came out into the main space again, I found the two people I was closest to in the world huddled around Vasily's laptop, both frowning. "This cannot be good," I said, putting my hand on Suzanne's back.

"I'm not sure," she said thoughtfully. "I knew this was an unusual death, but... wow."

"Yeah, caught under the seat."

Suzanne looked at me. "Yeah... about that," she said.

My masked eyes widened. "Uh oh."

"The coroner has left little wiggle room around *when* Chase died."

"Oh?" I asked, looking to Vasily. "We did have a thought that maybe Chase didn't make the phone calls himself but haven't locked that down yet."

"I'm not sure he could have," Suzanne said. "Admittedly, I didn't do the autopsy, so I am inferring based on what the ME observed. He seems to think the angle of the body is such that Chase would have been unable to ease the pressure against him at all – that the seat was forcibly pressed *down* on him almost all at once. He didn't do any investigation into that since there originally was no suspicion of foul play, but yeah." She looked up. "He would have been physically unable to draw a breath. That means maybe less than thirty seconds before he blacked out; two minutes, tops, before he was dead."

"He was an athlete," Vasily pointed out. "Isn't it reasonable to think he could have given himself a bit more time? Either by pushing up or because he was in such good shape?"

Suzanne tapped a finger on something in the report. "Perhaps," she said after a moment. "But to be honest, at best he might have bought himself an extra thirty seconds. At most, maybe a minute." She looked up at me. "But given the timeline Vasily told me, while it's *maybe* possible he called 9-1-1 the first time, there was no way he could have made the second."

"That is a lot of *maybes*," I pointed out. "What is your gut telling you?" I asked carefully.

She smiled. "The same as you, I think. He was quite dead before that first phone call was made."

I nodded. "Yep." I looked over to Vasily.

"Yes," he said. "There are multiple sets of prints on the car, all tie back to the family. But get this," he smiled crookedly, "there was one unknown print on the driver's side door, and on the back seat. About where you might put a hand were you pulling – or pushing – the seat."

"You did get the family printed?"

"I managed that much before getting shut down," he smiled. "I *had* planned on printing the car, too, but again, since the investigation ended practically before it began..."

I nodded again. "When is the panel you want to go to?" I asked Suzanne.

"We still have time for dinner," she hedged, a concerned look on her face. "Why?"

I pulled my cell phone out. "I need to talk to Mike," I smiled. "And Vasily needs to schedule a FaceTime call with Chase's parents."

"Will it take long?" she asked, frowning. "I kind of want to eat."

"I think we will be able to make dinner," I smiled, feeling better than I had in a long, long while.

Thirty-Two

Vasily and I were leaning against the chain link fence surrounding the tennis courts at Rancho Linda High School early the next morning when Dalton Ramsfeld came up the walkway carrying a basket of florescent green balls and a bag of rackets. He smiled a bit nervously when he saw us.

"Gentlemen," he said as he paused in front of us. "I wasn't expecting to see you again."

"Sorry to drop in unannounced."

"More questions?" he asked. "I'm not sure how much more I can tell you about Chase."

"Actually," I said, "I'd like to talk to you about Bobbie."

"Who?" he asked, a little too fast.

"I have to thank you, actually," I continued. "You're the one that mentioned Bobbie to us."

"I did?" he paused. "Oh," he said as if he were suddenly remembering something. "The photo in Chase's locker. His girlfriend? I guess?"

"Exactly," I nodded. "Except, he wasn't."

Dalton frowned. "Chase wasn't? What?"

"Not Chase," Vasily said. "Bobbie."

Dalton looked at us, and I could see him doing a mental calculation. It was one I'd often seen happen behind the eyes of people I investigated – how much of the truth could they tell and still not get into any personal hot water? How far could they claim innocence? And, more importantly, wondering what *exactly* we knew ourselves. That last part was always the gamble, and one that I generally encouraged them to make.

My hand was weak this time, though; under normal circumstances, I would go back for the warrant to obtain the video evidence from Disney, but I had a hunch if I threw down just the right cards, in the right sequence, I could get Dalton to fold. For at the core of this case, I felt, was a mistaken perception and, I hoped, a well of self–recrimination threatening to drown its victim.

"Do you want to go somewhere to talk?" I asked pleasantly. "Somewhere more private?"

"Practice is in a few minutes," he hedged, hoping he could stave off the inevitable.

"You might want to have your assistant coach take over," Vasily recommended.

Dalton looked at me, and then Vasily, gauging perhaps where this was going to go. He chose the truculent route, unfortunately. "This is fine right here."

"Okay," I nodded, looking to Vasily who inclined his head slightly. It was our common sign that he had activated the voice recorder on his iPhone.

"Dalton Ramsfeld, you have the right to remain silent…" Vasily started, reciting from memory the Miranda Warning. As he wrapped up, Dalton's eyes had grown wide. "Do you understand what I have told you?" Vasily asked.

"Am I being arrested?" he asked.

"We just need to be formal about how we ask our questions," I replied smoothly. "But if you want to head to the station with us, we can totally hook you up with a lawyer. I'd prefer to keep this pleasant, though."

Dalton looked at me. "Do I need a lawyer?"

"I can't tell you that," I replied with a smile. "Do you want one? Or are you waiving your right to a lawyer at this time?"

"I don't have anything to hide," Dalton replied. "I'm good."

Not likely, I thought, knowing he had committed the cardinal sin all guilty people made. They always seemed to think that if they simply ex-plained themselves, we'd understand their motivations, pat them on the back and send them on their way with a smile. The odds of that hap-pening with Coach Ramsfeld were somewhere between zero and zero.

"When did you find out Chase was dating Bobbie?" I asked.

"When I found the photo."

"I see. Chase didn't talk about her at all?"

"No," he said. "I mean, maybe? If he was telling his teammates, I may have overheard him. I don't really remember."

"I see," I repeated, looking to Vasily.

"Did you call Adele Cromwell at one point and warn her that Chase had lost his focus?"

Dalton blinked. "I... don't remember doing that, no."

"Funny," Vasily said as he flipped through his notes. "We talked with her last night. She recalls it rather vividly. Seems you warned her that his scholarship was in jeopardy, and that he needed to drop any outside distractions."

"I'm not—"

"That, actually, you pleaded with her to have him stop dating, and I quote, 'that misbegotten young man' before Berkeley pulled the plug?"

"No," he said firmly. "I mean, yes, Chase *had* lost his focus, but—"

"Isn't it true that you told her Berkeley would, in fact, dump his 'gay ass' if he pursued a relationship with Bobbie?"

"They would have!" he cried out suddenly, face flushed. "I would have insisted! We can't have someone *like that* representing Rancho Linda! No matter *how* talented he was!"

"Like *what*, exactly?" I asked calmly.

"You have to understand!" he pleaded with me. "Chase was the first four-star recruit this high school has ever had – in *any* sport! He rep-resented this community and had no idea the lifestyle he was pursu-ing jeopardized everything we'd been working toward." He paused for a long, long moment. "What he had to do was so simple! Just walk away. He didn't even need to get an actual *real* girlfriend – leaving that... that make-believe almost girl would have been the right move."

"I take it he refused," Vasily said impassively.

I turned, for as carefully neutral as his face was, I could see the fire behind his eyes. It matched my own fury, for I had assumed – incorrectly, it seems – that society had gone beyond such distinctions around sexuality. Love in my book was truly blind to everything, and none of us had any say in how each of us pursued it. Looking back at Dalton, I tried to keep the distaste I was feeling off my own face.

People like you should be relegated to the past, I thought angrily. *How could you have existed into this century? Where,* I demanded, *have we as a society failed you?*

The universe didn't deign to answer.

"He did," Dalton replied, kicking at the ball carrier as he answered. "In fact, if you can believe it, he tried to convince me he wasn't actually in love with Bobbie. He was just her friend." Dalton looked up. "I knew it was more than that. I caught him at that deviant bookstore over at the mall a few weeks ago, chatting with Bobbie and others."

"So, you started to monitor him?" I asked.

"I had to! I needed to know if he was crossing over."

"Doesn't he deserve the same right to privacy that you enjoy?" I asked pointedly. "I'm not sure any of us would appreciate someone looking over *our* shoulder."

"There was too much at stake," Dalton replied testily. "He was our *star*. Even the hint of impropriety would have jeopardized everything!"

I couldn't help the frown now. An adult following a student, even if he were of age, came perilously close to crossing other lines. Especially and adult in a position of power. "Stalking them to Disneyland seems out of bounds to me. Why did you do it?"

"I didn't—"

"We have you on tape," Vasily said with a slight lie of omission. "Why did you follow them?"

Dalton began to pace. "Okay! Fine. *Fine!* I followed them; I knew Chase had been going to that damn bookstore every Saturday before practice, and I was sitting in the mall parking lot watching. Waiting."

He looked up, anger inflaming his face. "They went in together as two guys. They came out as a couple. It was, to put it mildly, distasteful."

"You confronted them, then." It was more a statement on my part than a question.

"Yes. I insisted he rethink going to the park, being visible to the world like that! Someone might have seen them! What if it had landed on social media? The headlines were right there in front of me. 'Local tennis start outed at Disneyland.' It was disgraceful."

"And it worked," Vasily said icily. "You drove them both away from the Happiest Place on Earth."

"Yes," Dalton nodded. "But I knew they were just gonna go right back to those witches at the bookstore. I'd had it. I needed him to break away from all of it."

I didn't want to lead him, but I was growing ill from the conversation. "You staged an intervention?"

Dalton looked at me, his eyes wide with panic. "It wasn't my fault," he said.

"Okay," I nodded encouragingly. "Walk me through what happened."

Ramsfeld swallowed. "I followed them back to the bookstore, and oddly, Chase drove around behind the store – to the loading dock, I think. He parked the van, and I parked my car behind him."

"And waited?"

He nodded. "They went in together, but Chase came out alone. It was my moment, and I took it; he had gotten behind the driver's wheel, and I yanked the door open and grabbed him by the shirt. I wanted to talk! That's all I wanted to do."

"I take it he didn't want to talk. At all."

"No," Dalton said. "He squirmed out of my grasp and tried to get away from me. I tried to stop him – I just wanted to talk, you know? That's it!"

"Did you follow him into the van?"

"I needed to convince him! He wouldn't listen to me. Not at all!" Dalton started pacing again. "He tried to get away from me, to open the sliding door and escape, but I yanked it closed. He had to listen to me!"

"So he moved further away from you."

His eyes widened. "It wasn't my fault."

"What happened?" Vasily asked quietly.

Dalton increased his pacing. "He was trying to call someone. I don't know who. I had to have him listen to me! So I leaned over the seat to grab his phone from him. I'd just reached it when—"

He choked off. "It wasn't my fault!"

"The seat?" I prompted.

"It snapped down on top of him," he said after a moment. "He was dead before I knew what happened."

"You didn't even try to save him?" I asked, fury in my tone.

"He was gone," Dalton said, and I knew he was right. "But I did call for help. I had his phone in my hands, and realized what it might look like if I was found with him. So I put the phone up front, tapped 9–1–1 and ran back to my car."

"And left?"

Dalton paused. "No," he said. "I drove away and then came back. Conscience, I think; I needed to be there when they found him." He looked up at the sky. "Except no one came."

"Cellphones are hard to track," I told him. "Why did you call again?"

"No one came," he repeated sadly. "I went back to the car, dialed 9–1–1 again, but this time I didn't wait around. I left." Dalton looked up at us. "I found out later that somehow, his van wound up at the school hours afterward. I have no idea about that, but I am glad he was found, finally. But it wasn't my fault."

"You can keep telling yourself that," Vasily said. "And maybe the judge might believe it."

Dalton's eyes widened. "I'm not in trouble, am I?"

"Let's just say you're not going to be available for practice this morning," I said. "Or, perhaps, for a long, long time to come."

Thirty-Three

"My wife told me about Dalton's visit," Parker Cromwell's image on my MacBook told me. "And when I pinged Chase's phone and saw he was at *The Alternative Way*, I was afraid that maybe what Dalton had said was true." He paused, eyes brimming with tears. "I panicked and made a foolish mistake. But I thought it prudent to move him."

"You realize by moving the van, it hid the crime, right?" I said hotly. "The very investigation you demanded later would have started properly if you had not only left the van where you found it but had told all of this to someone like Detective Korsokovach in the first place."

"But I did tell someone, Sean," he said. "That first detective – Mark something – we told all of this to him; at least, as much as I was comfortable telling, for I knew what it would look like if I told him about moving the van. He assured us it would be looked into."

I sat back on the comfortable patio chair on Vasily's small balcony outside his apartment. Admittedly, it was a nice spot, albeit rather small; ever the gentleman, he'd decamped to the small pullout mattress from his loveseat so Suzanne and I could crash in his master suite and its king-sized bed. It was a lovely gesture, driven perhaps by practicality, given how crunched the two of us would have been on the pullout. Then again, he'd not planned on having houseguests.

"Another thing for us to follow up on," I said tiredly. "One last thing," I asked.

"Yes?"

"What did you hit when you backed out?"

Parker smiled wryly. "One of those bollards protecting the dumpster Chase had parked next to."

I nodded. "So, it wasn't inaccurate what you told us – the van did actually leave your house without the groove."

Parker smiled grimly. "Thirty years of perfect driving shot in thirty seconds."

"All right," I said as I rubbed my eyes. "That's it for now."

"Thank you," Parker said. "I can't tell you how much this closure means for us."

"I suspect they will charge Dalton," I nodded. "But Chief Gilbert will be taking it from here."

"Okay," he replied. "Have a safe flight home, Sean."

His image winked out and I turned to Vasily. "And that is *that*," I smiled.

"Save for the paperwork," he laughed. "But yes."

I looked at my friend of many years and felt a bit introspective. "It was nice to work with you again, Vas," I said as I picked up the beer that had been just off camera. "I don't know what will happen moving forward, but I miss having you as a partner." I smiled crookedly. "As complicated as our relationship is, and at the risk of making things messier... I, uh, miss *you*."

Vasily smiled a bit. "Same," he admitted. "In every way."

I took a sip from the bottle. "I had conflicting thoughts when I first arrived," I said. "And right up until I lost my job, I was considering asking you to return with me. I can't obviously do that now, of course, and I'm sure you wouldn't want to come back." I paused. "Right?"

Vasily looked at me, and then titled his whole head down to stare at the beer he was holding. He'd pulled his hair out of its normal ponytail, and it fell forward with the motion, obscuring his face for a moment. "I can't go back, Sean," he said softly. "All of the original problems between us remain." He sighed as he looked up, his eyes hidden slightly beneath his long blond bangs. "That's not entirely fair, I suppose, because it's not like they are *your* problems. They're all mine, and clearly, I've not been able to fix them. Despite moving out here, nothing has changed for me with respect to how I feel about you."

I smiled sadly. "You've not been away long enough to forget about me. Is that it?"

"Maybe," he replied as he took a swig from the bottle.

I looked at my friend, the man who meant more to me perhaps than anyone, including Suzanne; we had been together for so long, now, I couldn't imagine life without him in it. I knew I loved him – had for years, really – but now, for the first time, I could feel that it broke my own heart that it wasn't in the way he craved the most.

We'd been over that ground before multiple times, and even *thinking* about those conversations made me sad when I considered just how much I must be hurting him by *not* reciprocating in the way he desired.

But it seemed crueler to me to cleave our relationship in the way we had, separated by thousands of miles and a difference in feelings. If I had learned anything from the Hell of the last few months, it was that I hadn't appreciated fully how interdependent the two of us were. Vasily was right on one count: bringing him back to Maine did more for me than him. I grew angry with myself for even suggesting that option, given how one–sided it would have been.

"I'm sorry," I said softly. "I shouldn't have even broached the topic. It's not fair to you at all."

"Don't apologize," he smiled. "I am weak in all things Sean and would follow you anywhere you asked me to go." He blew a bang in despair. "It's my lot in life, I suppose. You are a dish I cannot resist, no matter how high the personal stakes might be."

"You make it sound so dramatic," I observed.

"For me, it is," he said as he drained the last of his bottle and set it on the table. "I'll be honest, I'm not really happy here. I miss what we had; we may not have been romantically involved, but we spent enough time together to have reached that intimate level of friendship few ever get the chance to experience."

I nodded. "We *have* that," I corrected. "Not past tense."

Vasily smiled. "I suppose you're right, considering how quickly we fell into our normal patterns together when you got here." He sighed again. "But returning with you to Maine feels like a step backwards to me. Even if my life sucks in Southern California."

Something inside me tore slightly. "I understand," I said as I sensed a sudden dread at returning without him. I wondered what it meant, given Suzanne would be there with me. There was something there I knew I didn't want to delve into for some reason. A gnawing deep within my soul that I was on the precipice of losing something very precious to me, perhaps for the second and final time.

It didn't feel right. But despite all of my years spent finding the right answer to any question, I was coming up empty in that department.

"What do we do now?" I asked as I toyed with my bottle. "Will you at least return my phone calls after this?"

"I might even call you from time to time," he laughed quietly. "Baby steps, Sean."

"I'm not sure I want to go that slow," I replied honestly.

"We'll settle out into an equilibrium again at some point," he said as he stood and took my now empty bottle and picked up his. "Another?"

"Yes," I said as I stood and walked to the railing. The balcony was off his living room and had a prime angle on nearby Disneyland; I could just make out the top of the Matterhorn and could see several spires of the castle, making me wonder how frequently he caught the regular fireworks display from the park. Below me, what Vasily had said was typical weekend traffic in Anaheim bustled by; to my eye, it looked barely removed from the worst rush hour I'd ever seen in Boston. Turning, I watched as Vasily pulled something from his fridge and marveled at how he'd turned the apartment into his home; there were small touches everywhere that undeniably made it his own.

When I'd first moved into the bungalow back in Windeport, I'd thought that would become my own version of that, but the space had never grown on me. It was lovely, of course, and the views of the ocean always centered me. Perhaps it was the simple aspect of having grown up along the coast that tied me to that spot, and yet all I felt was dread at returning.

It wasn't specifically because I had lost my job, though that was certainly a part of it. Facing an unknown future was new for me, but that really wasn't the core of my worry, either. Something had changed as a result of this trip to California, but my brain was still processing all of the details; either way, I had unfinished business back home that needed attending to. Once that was complete, I'd have plenty of time to hash out what was truly bothering me and make whatever decisions needed to be made about my future.

Vasily reappeared, not with two beers but glass tumblers rimmed with salt. "Figured you could use something a bit stronger," he said as he held out a margarita to me. "I know I did."

I smiled and accepted the gift, but not before tapping it to his glass. "Thank you, my friend. For this and for everything."

"It was the least I could do," he said as he took a sip from his glass. "You saved what is left of my sorry career in Rancho Linda. Not to mention all the times you bailed me out back home."

I shrugged. "That's what friends do," I said as I sampled the frosty beverage. The tequila had a bit of a bite to it that was a welcome surprise, and I was about to remark on it when my iPhone sang out a jaunty tune.

Putting the glass down with one hand, I picked the phone up with the other and felt my eyes widen at the number. "This could be interesting," I said as I swiped to accept the call.

"Who is it?" Vasily asked as I answered it.

"Caitlyn," I said both to him and to the woman at the other end of the line many thousands of miles away. "I didn't expect to hear from you again."

"Hey Chief," she said amicably. "I bring tidings of joy and good fortune."

"Oh?" I said, leaning back against the railing.

"Yeah. A few of us forced an emergency meeting of the Village Council on Friday, specifically in protest of the sudden dismissal of the Chief.

I won't lie, the meeting was rather acrimonious, but after multiple people spoke on your behalf, the Council was persuaded to review their action."

I felt an eyebrow go up. "A few?" I asked.

Caitlyn laughed. "Okay, it was standing room only. You have more friends here than you realize, Sean," she said softly. "More than enough to offset those corporate lawyers from away."

"I... had no idea," I said, feeling somewhat blindsided.

"It also helps that, per your contract, the Village would have to pay out a year and a half of salary to you if they terminate you prior to the end of your contract."

"Which they might well do in June," I observed.

"Maybe," she laughed again. "But I doubt they want to face the shitstorm they endured last night again." She paused and lowered her voice. "No one likes getting on Charlie's bad side, Sean. Even the town fathers know better."

I nodded. "Already on my to–do list," I said in response to her subtle rebuke.

"Anywho, I never did get around to cancelling your flight. So we'll see you back here Monday morning, right?"

"Yes," I smiled again. "Apparently you will."

"Good. All of us miss the smell of your Keurig in the morning," she laughed as she hung up.

I stared at my iPhone and turned to Vasily, a bit of a dazed look on my face. "What?" he asked, a partial question in his smile.

"It's good to be Chief," I laughed as I took a deep swig of the margarita.

"They reinstated you?" he asked.

"They did indeed," I said, smiling wider. "Too bad they didn't tell me before I accepted Mike's payment."

Vasily's eyes widened. "They don't know about the direct payment to you from Rancho Linda, do they?"

"Dinner is on me, my friend."

Thirty-Four

True to form, it was snowing when I turned off of Route One to drop Suzanne at her apartment. As I put the pitiful excuse of a sedan into park, I leaned over and kissed her, then asked: "Can I change in your apartment?"

She pulled away with a smile. "Of course," she replied a bit quizzically. "But why?"

"I'm heading to Charlie's after this," I said as I exited the car and popped the trunk to pull out her suitcase and my duffel. "I had a brainstorm on the flight out – a way to soften the impact of my sudden appearance on her porch."

Looking at my bag, she smiled wider. "That is playing dirty, Chief Colbeth. I thought you were a paragon of virtue."

"I *am*," I said as I kissed her again. "But I'm not above twisting the situation to my advantage, either."

Less than thirty minutes later, the tires of the sedan crunched as they rolled across the icy snow that had covered the rutted tracks leading to Charlie's turn–of–the–last–century farmhouse. The farm had been in her family for generations, and while she was no longer actively working the land, she did allow the next farm over to use the parts not acting as a tree farm so she could still afford the property taxes.

As I came to a stop at the base of the steps to the wide porch that fronted the farmhouse, I could see Charlie's two daughters building opposing snow forts on the wide swath of open land just below the house proper. It was hard for my brain to understand that I'd been jogging around in less than nothing a few hours earlier; the fifteen–degrees showing on the car's thermometer was a bit of a wakeup call that I was no longer in paradise.

I grabbed the baton in one gloved hand and my belt tail in the other, then slipped out of the car. The crisp air sliced through the thin layer of the Chat Noir costume, causing an involuntary shiver as I closed the door behind me and moved toward the porch. The girls saw me, hollered at each other, and then trundled across the snow as fast as the terrain allowed.

"Chat! *Chat!*" the younger of the twins cried as she bounded over the snowbank, sliding down on her backside before racing toward me. "Why are you here?"

I smiled, for it was still hard for me to believe the eight–year–old didn't recognize her uncle. "I am on a mission, and I need to see you mother. Is she home?"

"Yep!"She took my gloved hand and tugged me toward the porch, her sister just behind. "Wait here, I'll get her," she said excitedly as the two of them burst through the door into the farmhouse proper.

I stayed at the bottom of the steps, much as I had months earlier when I had confronted Charlie. Ignoring the icy cold wind that was sure to add a rosy glow to my cheeks, I started to idly twirl my tail as I waited. We'd taken a redeye flight out of Los Angeles and had made it back close to noon, East coast time; still, with the drive up from Port-land, I had less than an hour before the sun sank below the horizon and took the temperatures with it.

"Chat," I heard from above and behind me.

I turned, a slight smile on my face, and saw Charlie standing in the doorway wearing her flour–splattered apron. Her arms were crossed, and she was holding a wooden spoon in one hand, partially as a warn-ing, and partially to remind me there were more important things than talking with her cousin. "Madame," I said in my best faux French accent. "Might I have a private word with you?"

That smile quirked. "Come on in," she said, stepping back to allow me access.

Taking the steps two at a time, I managed to get through the door a fraction of a moment before she shushed her twins back out. "This is an important *private* conversation between us," she warned them as they protested.

"But *mom*," the slightly older twin whined. "We want to help on the secret mission."

Charlie looked to me. "I'll discuss it with Chat and, if I think it's safe, I'll let you help. Deal?"

The kids looked between me and their mother. "Deal."

"Shush," Charlie said as she closed the door on them before stepping toward me. "Cousin. Not the way I expected to see you again."

"I figured it was the *last* thing you expected," I smiled. "Which is why I did it."

"If you intended to throw me for a loop, you have," she laughed as she waved me to a wing tipped chair beside her warmly worn couch with her spoon. "To what do I owe this honor?" she asked as she sat next to me.

"I am sorry," I said simply. "For what I put you through. I could have made it a bit easier, but I misjudged the situation. Vasily or someone else should have handled your interview." I sighed as my masked eyes searched hers. "I was admittedly desperate to get to the truth – to clear you, in fact – that I rode roughshod over you in the process. It wasn't my intent at all."

Looking away, I let my eyes fall on the watercolors her mother had painted years ago; she still created the seascapes and sold them in her restaurant along Route One, but these were more personal scenes from around the farm twenty years earlier. Much like her daughters, Charlie and I had conducted hundreds of snowball fights on the grounds below the house while our parents visited; summers had been spent together swimming in the small river that bordered her property to the next and ran all the way out to the ocean.

"I know you were one of the most vocal people who stood up for me at the Village Council meeting," I said as I turned my masked visage back upon her. "While I don't know exactly what you and the others said, I am overwhelmed with the generosity. Especially given how I've been treated over these last few months."

Charlie chuckled. "Small town mentality, Cousin. You know that. We hold a grudge until something even more righteous outweighs it. We, collectively, might have been pissed off about *how* you conducted the investigation, but we also can't argue with the results, either. And your track record both here and statewide speaks for itself." She laughed again. "Just because a certain university dean still has some pull – even from prison, it seems – doesn't mean she has a right to try and crush your career."

She paused and then smiled, the warmth I'd come to love visible once more in her expression. "Besides, the kids have missed you," she said before pausing. "I've missed you," she added quietly.

"Same," I said, feeling the sting of tears in my eyes and seeing the matching glistening in hers.

"You'll stay for dinner," she stated as she stood and began to usher me to her massive kitchen. "I'm making my chili tonight."

I smiled as I got up to follow her. "I *was* hoping I'd softened you up enough with the costume."

"You did," she replied. "But you have one last act of penance before I will completely forgive you."

"Oh?" I asked as I arched a masked eyebrow. "And what is that?"

"The girls will enjoy dinner with their superhero idol, I think."

My masked eyes widened. "Charlie! I can't eat with these claws!"

"You'll find a way," she laughed. "Come on, I've got a bottle of red open that I'll share to help ease your pain."

Thirty-Five

⚛

Epilogue

I had never fully understood the concept of daylight savings, other than to accept it was simply a part of life. When it was moved even earlier into March, I complained as bitterly as anyone else about getting up for Masters swim practice in the dark and then returning home after work under pitch black conditions. However, I couldn't deny the silver lining when May rolled around and I was able to sneak out for a run on a Saturday in full sunlight, despite it only being five in the morning.

While I'd returned to the Masters team after the mutual town healing a few months earlier, I'd gotten used to *not* swimming on Saturdays, instead alternating that workout time for weight training or runs. The Saturday of Memorial Day weekend happened to be a running day, and found me lacing up my sneakers on the front porch before heading out for an easy ten kilometers around Greater Windeport. To be honest, it was likely the last time I'd be able to use this particular route for Main Street would be nigh near impossible to cross once the tourists descended on us – even at that ungodly hour.

Suzanne would normally spend Friday night at my place, but she had been in Portland for the last few days watching over a patient who'd had a serious stroke earlier in the week. While not strictly her specialty, as the general practitioner on record she'd felt obligated to keep her hand in their treatment. I'd planned on braving I–95 later that day to join her for the rest of the long weekend at the Marriott she'd been staying in, with the added bonus of treating her to dinner at DiMillo's that evening. I'd not been to that floating restaurant in a few years, and had made reservations to ensure we could get in on such a busy weekend.

My mind wandered as I went on automatic, circumnavigating the village while only partially paying attention to my surroundings. A little less than forty minutes later, I rounded the corner to my small neighborhood and found myself slowing a bungalow from my own. An extremely familiar Camaro that I'd not seen in months was parked along the curb in front of my carport; despite having California plates, it had the air of *belonging* right where it was. I couldn't help how eagerly my eyes sought out the long, blond hair of the person sitting on my porch steps; pulled back into a quasi–ponytail, it was more disheveled than I would have ever expected.

I picked up my pace and hurried down the curve of the road, running right to the bottom of my steps where I pulled up and stopped the workout on my watch. "Vasily?" I asked, taking in the wrinkled polo and shorts. A small duffel bag was behind him on the porch.

Oddly, he was wearing overly large sunglasses that were totally not his style; my investigator radar went into overdrive and my eyes started to assess him differently. I could feel a frown creasing my face as I saw a faint outline around his throat. I had been in law enforcement long enough to recognize the evidence of attempted manual strangulation. Without asking, I moved closer; Vasily flinched, but didn't object when I pulled the sunglasses off, revealing the remains of a significant black eye. He looked as though he'd been in one Hell of a prize fight.

"This would be a good time to tell me how the other guy looks," I said as I slid his glasses back up. "But something tells me that your unexpected arrival on my doorstep means it's far more complicated than that."

"It is," he said, his voice gravelly. "Suffice it to say," he started again, swallowing hard to try and talk, "my last relationship didn't end well. Especially for him."

I raised my eyebrows. "What the hell happened?"

"I'd... I'm not quite ready to talk about it," he said hoarsely. "But more immediately, I've been placed on indefinite leave. I... needed to get away from all of it." He looked up at me. "You were the first person I thought of. I'm sorry..." he swallowed again, the act of speaking clearly painful. "I should have called."

"You are always welcome," I reminded him. "No matter what. You know that. But you look like shit."

He smiled slightly. "I drove straight through. It was the only thing I could afford on short notice."

My eyes widened. "That's like... what? Four days?"

"Three and change," he croaked. "Not an experience I care to repeat."

I took the spot next to him on the steps. "Stay as long as you like," I said, "and when you are ready, I want every last detail. If the guy that did this to you is who I *think* it is—"

"It is," Vasily said very quietly.

"—then I'm gonna track down the bastard and—"

"He's dead," Vasily interrupted. "Hence why I am on leave."

"Oh," I said.

"Exactly," he rasped.

"Well," I continued, "my offer stands. Stay as long as you like."

"Thank you." Vasily leaned back, relaxing slightly in the sunshine. For the first time since he'd appeared on my doorstep, he looked more comfortable. "Any sense of normalcy is better than what I've lived through over the past few weeks."

"Come on," I said as I stood. "I've got some warmups you can use and a brand–new hot water heater. Get cleaned up and we'll go down to Calista's for pancakes."

"*That* is the best offer I've had in days."

"It won't be the last," I said with a vengeance. "Not by any stretch."

Acknowledgement

They say the second book is easier than the first. I'm not entirely sure that is true, for at least in my case, it felt like my characters had some definite ideas about who they were and what they wanted to do; often, they rather stubbornly refused to follow my carefully constructed outline, much to my consternation.

I'm also not certain that handing off a *second* book to your trusted group of beta readers is any less nerve wracking than the first, especially now that there is a shared history and a (quasi) shared understanding of the nascent universe being created. It makes it all the more important to have friends and colleagues who'll tell it to you straight – whether you want to hear it, or not.

As I write this, I've penned four novels in this series, and as I embark on the fifth, I know for sure the wise observations, suggestions and, yes, even corrections have made my stories even better. I cannot say *thank you* enough to these amazing people:

Charlotte, Tristan and Lisa, aka the **Writing (S)quad of Doom**: once more, you were there for the random, non-sensical questions thrown at you in the middle of the night, and to properly bash me for Sean's incessant caffeine intake and fondness for a certain fruit.

Kristin: your well-timed validation that my perception of today's high school students was on the mark meant more to me than you know.

And of course, my wife, **Paula**: poignant observations and a shrewd suggestion helped smooth out the early part of this narrative – and gave me an insane idea for book four. I am nothing without your quiet support. As I said at the end of the first book: you are my muse and my biggest fan, and there is absolutely no way I could have done this without you. My love is yours, always and forever.

-- C

February 6, 2021

About the Author

Born and raised in Maine, Chris has spent nearly three decades as an IT nerd, writing just about everything *other* than a novel in the process. That changed in early 2019 when he was advised to find a way to wind down from his day job; sifting through his options, he recalled a childhood ambition to become a writer and quickly found himself weaving an entirely new world from the comfort of his laptop. *Outsider* is his second book, part of a planned series featuring both Chief Sean Colbeth and Detective Vasily Korsokovach.

Despite his love for the Northeast, the author escaped the cold for Arizona, where he currently resides with his beautiful wife, two cats, and a Shar-Pei mix that insists on being walked regularly.

Much to his surprise, the author now has a website! Follow along for all of the latest information at https://chrisjansmann.com.